QUEEN TAKES MORE

JOELY SUE BURKHART

Queen Takes More

A Their Vampire Queen Compilation
By Joely Sue Burkhart

You wanted more. More Shara. More blood. More *Blood*.

You had so many questions after Shara Isador took the Triune. Why was Daire in the cathouse? Why didn't she get immediate revenge against the Dauphine? These questions are answered, along with providing all of the Their Vampire Queen short stories that were previously published in other anthologies, including:

Queen Takes Alpha

Queen Takes Twins

Queen Takes a Late Christmas

And since you're all so very greedy, there's some additional time for Okeanos in this compilation. Of course, it's appropriately titled Queen Takes Tentacles.

For my Beloved Sis.

Thank you to my comma warriors and beta readers:

Sherri Meyer, Stephanie Cunningham,
Lydia Simone, Bibiane Lybæk, Kaila Duff, and Jennifer Swan

QUEEN TAKES IT OUT ON ME

Special thanks to Cheyenne Boatman for the
perfect tribute song
(Set after Queen Takes Triune)

DAIRE

"**E**vidently, you don't trust me at all."

Her words made me flinch. My purr died in my chest. I risked a quick glance at my queen's face, and yeah, she was pissed.

But worse…

She was fucking *hurt*.

Her eyes gleamed with tears, and her bond weighed heavy inside me like cold, hard lead.

She hadn't been quite right since the Dauphine sent her mother's zombie to the nest. Goddess, who wouldn't have been shaken by that? She'd had to deal with the body and release Selena's spirit. It must have been like losing and burying her all over again, though she hadn't been able to attend her mother's funeral. She'd fled Kansas City after her mother's murder and never looked back.

We'd barely been back from Rome a few hours. She hadn't even gone upstairs to sleep yet, too wired after the encounter with Marne Ceresa.

I pressed harder against Shara's knees, but I couldn't purr. It was stuck deep in my chest, trapped like a wild thing that hammered inside me.

Any other time, she would have dropped her hand to my head and played with my hair. She would have smiled at my antics and jokes. I could have winked at her, flashed my dimples, and all would be forgiven. "Forgive me—"

"I don't want to hear it," she broke in.

Of course she knew that it wasn't a sincere apology. How could it be, when I had no idea what I'd done?

"I've done everything for you. I've bled. I've risked my life over and over. I walked into Heliopolis and let the sun god lay his creepy hands on me, so I could get close enough to him to use the red serpent. I drained Keisha Skye in her own court, simply because I had to protect you and Rik. I'd never let her claim one of you."

With each sentence, her words came faster, pouring out of her in a flood, as if she'd been holding back for too long.

"Worse, I had to go to Rome and endure Marne's polite-as-fuck insults. I stood in the midst of her power, completely helpless. I couldn't touch my own power. I couldn't call down fire to punish her. I couldn't do *anything*. Because the last thing I'd ever do is risk you. If another arrow or spear was shot into one of you... I would have lost everything, because I would have razed Rome to save you. Any one of you. And then Marne would have had us all legally executed and no one would have been able to lift a finger to stop her."

She paused a moment, taking a deep breath. "Don't you

fucking think I *wanted* to kill her? It certainly would have been easier. She hurt Rik, and I wanted her dead. It was all I could do not to call on my power and strike her down. Even if I'd killed her, we would have lost, because our goddesses don't want *any* of Their Triune queens to die. They need all three Triunes whole and strong, even if that means Marne and the Dauphine still live. I didn't know why. I still don't. I just know it was important and it had to be done. No matter the cost to my pride. I'd sit there and drink an ocean of tea and green snot in a bowl, if that meant I could save you and please the Great One at the same time."

I writhed helplessly against her knees, unable to bear the lash of her words.

"So for you to doubt me like this..."

Her voice broke and tears burned my eyes. I clutched her knees, leaning hard against her. Trying to soothe her with my body. "I don't doubt you, my queen. I'd never—"

"You do," she retorted. "You doubt me. *Me.* Or you would have come to me with this issue long before."

I couldn't bear her disappointment. It was horrible. I would rather she tell Rik to drag me outside by my hair and let his rock troll pound me into the ground than let her down.

I looked up at my alpha, but his face was devoid of even one iota of sympathy. Mouth tight and harsh, he didn't have to yell at me. His silence said it all.

The rest of her Blood were equally silent, their bonds ranging from grim acceptance to outright glee. Fucking Mehen was thinking really hard about popping a bag of popcorn.

I scowled at him and opened my mouth, but Shara cut me off, holding up her index finger. "You nearly made inappropriate jokes in front of a Triune queen, when you're supposed to be my gifted diplomat."

I winced, shame darkening my face. That had been especially stupid. Marne was already determined to find any reason at all to punish my queen, and I'd nearly put us at a disadvantage. And for what? A joke?

She lifted another finger. "You ridiculed a fellow Blood's need, when not one of us have ever ridiculed anyone because of a kink or desire." Another finger. "You interfered in a private moment with Nevarre when I didn't invite you to join us. Shall I go on?"

Miserable, I hung my head, fully contrite. "No, my queen. I'm ashamed of my behavior."

"Yet you still don't know why you behaved like a spoiled brat, do you?"

Her tone indicated it wasn't an actual question, but I shook my head anyway.

In all the months I'd served her, I'd only felt so awful one other time. When I'd considered hurting the cobra queen to save Rik. I'd paid dearly for that mistake and I thought I'd learned my lesson.

"Look at me, Daire."

My warcat rolled and wrestled inside me. Claws shredded my liver and his tail lashed my ribcage. It took me several tries to finally lift my head and meet her gaze.

Braced for anger, or worse, disappointment, the hint of wicked amusement in her eyes made my heart skip a beat.

"If you wanted me to punish you, all you had to do was ask."

SHARA

Daire's mouth fell open, his beautiful eyes heating like molten chocolate. And yeah, I was tempted to bend down and snag that delectable full lip between my teeth.

I knew he was into pain and punishment. That was one reason he loved to have one of my guys fuck him. They were bigger and meaner and stronger than I could ever be, at least in the physical department.

I'd never actually punished him before. I'd never deliberately hurt him… just because he wanted it. Because *I* wanted it. My subconscious mind must have been playing out scenarios, though, because I immediately had all kinds of ideas to try.

But I was actually very tired, drained and weary at a soul level. I ached all over, like I'd been run over by stampeding elephants, even though the confrontation with Marne Ceresa had been mostly verbal sparring. It'd still been mentally exhausting, and a tension headache threatened to crawl up the back of my head and spread pain to my temples.

I needed to recover some of my own energy first before I'd be up for any kind of punishment scene.

"Please, my queen. Please do your worst to me."

I settled back against Rik, drawing in his heat and strength against my back. I hadn't even changed out of the formal presentation gown yet. I needed to take it off and put it away before we damaged it, but I didn't want to get up. Not yet. Besides, the formal gown added another layer to this scene playing out. I'd never dressed up in royal clothes for my Bloods' enjoyment. Usually we were too busy taking my clothes *off*.

But sitting in my favorite chair with Rik wrapped around me, dressed in a glorious, expensive gown, with my crown on my head…

Yeah. I was a fucking queen. And Daire needed to be reminded of it.

Truth be told, so did I.

Meeting Marne had shaken me ways I hadn't even fully

reconciled in my head yet. I'd walked away from it unscathed, at least on the outside, but...

She'd rattled my confidence.

At the time, I'd been so clear with what I needed to do. What better way could I get my revenge on the Dauphine than by leaking her location to her greatest enemy? Not just her location, but also the method in which she hid herself. It was the kind of move a Triune queen would make.

The kind of move neither of them would ever expect from an upstart, impetuously young queen full of herself and her heritage.

I'd known dealing with the Triune queens would be a different kind of game than any of the other queens I'd met so far. But it still felt anticlimactic in some ways. No one had died. I hadn't destroyed Rome or brought down fire on the Dauphine's head.

Not yet.

Honestly, maybe never. As much as I hated the Dauphine for what she'd done to Mom, as soon as I even thought about blasting her, I felt a heaviness in my heart. An iron weight crushed my chest. Dread churned my stomach. The hairs prickled on my scalp, my nerves zinging with anxiety.

Not confidence. Certainly no assurance from Isis that I should proceed.

I won, I reminded myself firmly. *I upheld the Great Mother's will. We're too few and precious at this point.*

A sweet, high chime rang in my head. Confirmation from the goddess.

No more queens could die. We couldn't afford to lose any more ground. I knew it. Even though I didn't know *why* it was so important, or what dire threat may be approaching that even the Dauphine and the queen of Rome would need to be my allies.

Rik gripped the back of my neck in a hand powerful

enough to crush granite. Tenderly, he kneaded the tension ratcheting my shoulders and neck tighter. Gently but firmly, he worked his fingers up my nape. Stroked the back of my scalp, rubbing away the pain threatening to settle behind my eyes. Then back down to my shoulders.

"I have a suggestion, my queen," he said in a low rumble against my ear meant to carry to the man kneeling before me. "Let your Blood use him while you watch."

Use him. It was such an ugly way to suggest they all take a turn.

But Daire's eyes went heavy and dark at those words. He liked that idea. Very much indeed.

I didn't agree immediately. I'd never make anyone do anything they didn't want.

"Please," Daire whispered urgently. "Let them all use me. Let them punish me. I'll love it. The thought that you're watching…"

He paused, his breathing loud. His pupils were dilated, his sultry lips parted invitingly.

I raised my gaze to the rest of my Blood, gauging their interest in this proposed punishment. Vivian gave me a disgusted snort and shook her head. I knew she'd be out. Smoak shimmered around her shoulders, and I didn't have to listen to her bond to know the phoenix would definitely be willing to hop to me so I could fuck Daire like I'd fucked Nevarre.

"Hell yeah," Ezra said immediately, at the same time that Mehen snapped, "I'm first."

"Like hell you are," my bear retorted.

But my Templar knight surprised me when he stepped closer to us and started unbuttoning his jeans. Ezra and Mehen both loved Daire, but I didn't know Guillaume had ever had interest in fucking any man.

Pretending I'd offended him, he arched a brow at me as

he jerked his pants open. "I'm interested in fucking anyone and anything that will give you pleasure. I think size should go before everyone else, don't you, my queen?"

Mehen opened his mouth to argue, but grimaced. "I have him on age, but not on size. Sadly. Well, D, it was nice knowing you. The knight's going to rip you a new asshole."

One of my more quiet and reserved Blood, Tlacel raced out of the room. For a moment, I was afraid we'd terrified him, but he quickly returned with a hank of rope in his hands. "This is punishment, right, my queen? So he shouldn't be able to touch any of us, or gain any enjoyment by fighting back."

Of course, another submissive man would completely understand Daire's needs—and know how best to help us satisfy them. Because he was right. Listening to Daire's bond, I could feel the heat pulsing in his blood. He was rock hard, painfully aroused, ready for anything. Even my Templar knight's stallion-sized dick.

I winced at the thought of taking him anally. But Daire was panting, his eyes dark and shining as he stripped off his clothes in record time. "Take it all out on me. Everything. I can take it."

Tlacel looped the rope around each of Daire's wrists, crossed in the small of his back. But he didn't stop there. He made snug loops around the rest of Daire's torso, pulling the rope tight enough that his skin bulged through the coils.

Controlled. Bound. Maybe even painful, but not enough to injure him.

Blood splattered Daire's back, mesmerizing me. Gleaming red rubies on white rope and pink flesh. I licked my lips, my fangs throbbing as they descended. I followed the path of droplets, down the small of his back to the rounded globes of his ass as Guillaume lubed him.

My knight held his left wrist over Daire's ass, dripping

blood over him. Over himself. He lazily pumped his cock in his other hand, smeared with blood. Hunger suddenly spiked inside me, a raging wildfire of thirst that would never be quenched. I'd fed on all my Blood dozens, if not hundreds, of times in the few short months they'd been mine. I'd drained them to unconsciousness.

And it would never be enough.

Rik curled his left forearm around before my mouth, and it was all I could do not to immediately tear into his wrist and splatter myself with his blood. But it was much too early in our play to make my alpha come so quickly. He wasn't a jealous alpha by any means, but generally, Rik was the one to finish our lovemaking sessions if at all possible. I suspected that he wanted to be sure I was always satisfied, and deep down, he only trusted himself to ensure I was fully sated.

Even with eleven other Blood eager to make me come as many times as possible while they took their own pleasure.

My fangs throbbed, but I didn't sink them into Rik's wrist. Scenarios played out in my head, my brain leaping from one idea to the next in rapid-fire. Who did I wish to reward by bringing them closer? Who wouldn't mind playing, even if only a minor role from the sidelines? Who would Rik not mind biting him?

:I wouldn't mind anyone's bite as long as you feed, my queen.:

Mentally, I gave myself a shake. I didn't want to be this kind of queen.

A queen who played games. Even sexual games.

A Triune queen.

Fuck. I'm on the Triune. How much will things change now?

Llewellyn stepped closer, drawing my attention as he dropped to his knees on my left. "A powerful queen always plays games, especially with her pleasure and her blood. It's inevitable as you grow in power and call more of us to your side. Even you couldn't fuck twenty or thirty Blood at once, my queen. You will always need to choose who to reward with your presence, for we're greedy as fuck."

Deep down, there was a part of me that snorted defiantly and said, *"oh yeah, wanna bet?"*

A deep, guttural cry drew my gaze to Daire. On his knees, he'd leaned forward, his face pressed against his crossed arms. Bracing himself. As Guillaume started to work his ass open. My knight's face was hard with concentration. Controlling himself as he eased inside, stretching Daire's tight ass open.

"Oh no you don't." Guillaume muttered, fisting a hand in Daire's shaggy hair and jerking his head back. "Let her see the look on your face. Show her what a good kitty cat you are."

Even the scent of Rik's blood couldn't tear my gaze from the look on Daire's face as my knight worked himself deep. Enraptured pain. Agonized bliss. Sweat glistened on his forehead, his sandy-brown hair dark and damp. Eyes wide open and dark, he stared up at me. Breaking, slowly, before my eyes. Wall after wall coming down. Rubble dropping around him. Leaving him bare. Vulnerable.

Torn down to the bare studs. Exactly what he'd needed the most.

Rik pressed a bleeding bite to my mouth, careful to keep his beefy arm low so I could still watch. Llewellyn pressed along my side, not moving away now that he'd drawn Rik's blood for me. He kissed along my arm, his tongue flicking against every sensitive hollow, bringing my skin alive.

Shadows flickered across Daire's face. Muscles twitched along his jaws. His breathing rasped loudly and he bit his lip. Adding the scent of his blood to the air that seemed to shimmer all around me.

Heat. Energy. Blood. The entire room hummed with lust and pain and hunger.

Ezra knelt beside Daire and gripped his chin, keeping his head up. The sharp crack of his palm on Daire's hip made me jolt against Rik, but I didn't lift my mouth from his blood. "Don't hold back your cries and screams, D. We want to hear everything."

Daire whimpered, too softly for Ezra, evidently, because he gave him another sharp blow.

"Maybe you need my belt."

"Fuck that shit," Mehen growled, dropping down on Daire's other side. "Teeth work better than any flimsy piece of leather."

He curled over Daire's back enough to sink his fangs into the top of his shoulder. He shuddered and cried out, his voice rising in volume as Guillaume shoved to the hilt.

"Fuck." G grunted, jerking Daire's head back harder, straining his throat in a hard arc. "That's good, cat. You're stuffed to the whiskers now. I'd ask the lizard to stuff your mouth too, but I'd rather you see our queen and watch what the rest of us do for her while you're busy satisfying us."

Green eyes blinked up at me, sparkling with malice and glee as Mehen lifted his head. He jammed fangs into Daire's throat. His biceps. Not little love bites, but deep, hard strikes that left rivulets of blood dripping down the man's body. Each time, Daire cried out softly, his body shaking. Then he'd groan and shift again, trying to find some quarter from Guillaume's advance. But my knight had no mercy, inexorably shoving deeper.

Rocking back on his heels, he pulled Daire upright, keeping him skewered on his lap. Daire's cock was painfully hard, the head purple. Even before Tlacel started wrapping the end of the rope around him. The more Daire whimpered and shifted, the louder his cries became. Deep, guttural moans that made me shift against Rik.

I gulped his blood so hard that I almost choked and spluttered blood all over myself. My alpha was always semi-erect, but now he felt like a rock-hard column against my buttocks.

I wasn't aware that Llewellyn had tugged my bodice down, until I felt his tongue wrap around my nipple. I moaned around Rik's wrist, arching my chest up invitingly. Xin dropped beside us on my other side, adding his tongue to the exquisite torment.

Hands glided up my thighs. Sliding the heavy satin and silk skirts aside. Baring my pussy for the man being punished. And it was punishment for Daire. To be so close... but unable to touch. To smell my desire and see the cream welling from my core, and be unable to taste it. To know that my other Blood were touching me. Kissing me. Stroking my heat.

And he couldn't. He couldn't do anything but groan and take another inch of Guillaume's dick.

So many hands and mouths. Dazed, I couldn't focus on anything but the sensation of my Blood. They kept their touch soft and light, fingertips barely skimming my skin. Making goosebumps race along my limbs. Fangs delicately scratching—but not penetrating.

Rik's fingers slid inside me. I knew his touch. I would always know his hands from the others.

I released his wrist, letting my head fall back against his chest. He cradled me on his lap, one hand wrapped over my pussy, his other supporting my head as he lifted me up slightly. Giving my Blood better access, so they could carefully strip the court gown off my body.

Burning cinnamon filled my mouth. Vivian's lips locked to mine. Her burning-silk hair brushed my cheek. Someone's mouth closed over my clit, while Rik slowly stroked inside me. Nevarre, I thought. I could have used the bond to know for sure... but it was so erotic trying to decide just by touch. The weight of a hand, the way their tongues flicked or flattened or teased. Each one of them had such a different personality and presence.

"Please," Daire growled out, making me blink and focus on his face. He twisted harder against Guillaume, his eyes locked on my pussy. On Nevarre's dark head and Rik's hand.

Ezra slapped Daire's hip again, a sharp crack that made him buck in Guillaume's lap. "See, but don't touch. That's your punishment, D. Much worse than getting fucked by the hell horse, ain't it."

Someone picked up my right foot, his mouth hot on my ankle. My calf. The aggressive rasp of his tongue told me it was Mehen. Evidently he'd tired of biting Daire.

An image filled my head of them all feeding on me at once. I shuddered, desire spiking hard and fast inside me. I didn't have to ask. They were all entwined inside my head. They knew my thoughts almost before I could comprehend them myself.

Mehen sank his fangs deeply into my calf without hesitation. His fingers tightened on my ankle, holding me despite the involuntary kick and twitch. It hurt so good. The searing glide of ivory into that muscle. The heat and pressure of his mouth. Llewellyn and Xin both sank their fangs into my breasts, holding my throbbing nipples on their tongues. Vivian took my throat. Rik, my shoulder. Tlacel bit my other calf. Itztli curled my arm around him, so as he sank his fangs into my biceps, my nails would jab into his back. Nevarre didn't need my blood. Not when he was feasting from my core.

Pleasure pumped through me, looping through our bonds and slamming back into me magnified by my Bloods' feeding. Lost in sensation, I tried to do a mental count and see who was left. Who wasn't touching or feeding on me—or participating in Daire's punishment.

Okeanos. My newest Blood. I reached for him through

the fledgling bond. He came closer at once, taking my left hand in his. He didn't say words. He didn't have to. I could feel his heart and soul brushing mine.

He didn't want to intrude. He didn't know his place yet.

:This is your place,: I whispered in his mind, curling my fingers in his hair. *:With me. With us. Any way that you'd like.:*

He kissed the fragile, tender skin of my wrist, but he didn't feed. Again, I sensed a mental hesitation. As if he didn't have the right. Gently, I sank deeper into his mind as if floating on my back in my grotto. Lazily stroking my fingers through the endless dark water that flowed inside him.

Deep, dark and cold. Resigned, he waited for the chains. He waited for me to imprison him in the grotto beneath my heart tree. Evidently, even his mother had kept him imprisoned, fearful of his power as a king kraken.

My heart broke for him all over again. He'd never known freedom. Family. Belonging. Safety.

And yeah, a large part of him yearned for solitude. The peace and quiet of his deep secret place, rather than this loud and boisterous group of Blood. Even walking on two legs with the drying sting of air on his skin was an uncomfortable sensation.

He needed time. Both for his skin to adjust to being out of the water... and to having people in his life who cared about him and wanted to include him in daily interactions.

:Please, feed, my kraken. I want to deepen our bond, and you barely had a taste of me in Rome.:

His lips trembled against my skin, his heart flooding with emotion. Shock and elation and fear all swirling together. He wasn't afraid of me... but of adjusting to a new life with me, and then losing me when I banished him to a prison cell at the bottom of the ocean.

Like everyone else had done to him his entire life.

I wrapped my fingers around his nape, gripping firmly. *:I*

will never imprison you. Do you understand me? This queen never lies. I never break my word. What I love, I take, and what I take, I keep for all time. You are mine, Okeanos. Mine. I will never lock you away from me. You're safe now.:

:*Safe,:* he repeated softly, rolling the word around in his head. :*I don't really know what that means.:*

:*I'll show you.:*

DAIRE

With one last heavy thrust, Guillaume came inside me in a hot flood I could almost taste. Even spent, it took him a few moments to pull out of me.

Leaving me empty and aching on the floor at my queen's feet.

He gave my ass a friendly slap and then made his way to Shara, dropping back to his knees and wedging himself in between Llewellyn and Itztli so he could sink his fangs into her.

Ezra left me too, shoving in beside Tlacel so he could feed from her thigh.

On my belly, I scooted closer to her. Desperate to get my mouth on her. Even her pinky toe. I'd take it. I'd take anything that she gave to me. I was too low to reach her. No matter how hard I strained, I couldn't get my shaking legs beneath me. Not without the use of my arms.

Her desire crested again, scorching heat to lay waste to the entire earth.

And I could do nothing but lie on the floor and weep. With regret. Pain. And yes, relief. Because she'd given me exactly what I needed.

Even if I didn't like it.

Panting, I rolled over onto my side so I could at least look up at her, though her other Blood blocked most of my view. She lay on her back, fully suspended among the many hands eager to cradle her. I couldn't see for sure, but it was easy to guess that Rik was holding her head, leaving the rest of her Blood to support her body. She moved and rocked, body surfing on her Bloods' hands.

It was so fucking beautiful. Even if all I could do was watch and ache to touch her.

Finally Rik stood and gathered her closer against his chest. "Nevarre, bring up her gown, crown and shoes."

"Of course, alpha."

"G, organize the guard shifts. I want at least one winged Blood in the air every hour of the day and night, and at least three roaming the grounds outside the grove. We won't be surprised by another of the Dauphine's tricks."

Shara's arm hung down limply, her head lolling slightly as Rik carried her past me. She'd fallen asleep or passed out. All her Blood—except me—had fed on her. If they'd drained her…

I strained up higher, scrambling helplessly on the floor. Trying to get my head up high enough for her dangling fingers to touch me.

Rik, the fucking bastard, just kept right on walking. Didn't even pause or lower her down an inch to let me feel even the slightest brush of her fingers.

My dick throbbed like all nine circles of Dante's Inferno had taken up residence in my groin. If I didn't get that fucking rope off soon, she might have to heal me and see if a queen's blood could regrow a warcat dick.

Something snagged the rope binding my elbows together and lifted me, swinging me around effortlessly like a sack of meal. Rik dragged me along beside him like I weighed nothing, even carrying our queen in his other arm. He didn't say a word, but hauled me up the stairs. Frantically stumbling along, I tried to get my feet under me so I could limp alongside him rather than be dragged.

Inside her bedroom, he picked me up and tossed me face down on her bed. Luckily I managed to catch myself on my knees enough to roll slightly and protect my erection. I sure as fuck didn't want to hear Mehen's taunts if I broke my dick. I couldn't see much behind me, but I heard the quiet rustling as Nevarre put her dress away. The low murmur of their voices. I felt the slight dip in the mattress as Rik lay her down onto the bed.

Immediately, I turned my head, ready to roll toward her, but Rik seized my bound arms and pinned me in place. His big hands checked the ropes up my arms and chest, making my poor tortured dick throb even harder.

Goddess, I loved Shara more than life itself, but if I could have Rik fuck me too… I could die a very happy man.

He lifted me up enough to check the tortured condition of my dick and let out a low grunt. "Nevarre, grab her pocketknife."

"Sure thing, alpha."

I shivered and closed my eyes. Her knife. The only weapon she'd carried when we first found her. It would be absolutely perfect to have that knife free me. The only thing that could possibly make it better…

Groggy and gorgeously rumpled, Shara sat up and took the knife from Nevarre as he neared.

Goddess, thank you. Even unspoken prayers come true.

"What's the best way to do this?" Lips quirking, she lay the cold steel on my thigh. "I don't want to nick something important."

Rik manhandled me around, smashing my face down in the comforter. "Cut here. I'll unwind for you."

He applied enough pressure to my wrists to make my muscles scream with strain. I tried not to make a sound, but the heavy drag and jerk of the blade through the ropes made me whimper.

Her hair trailed over my fingers as she leaned closer. "That sound..." She licked her lips, making me whimper again. "I'm very hungry, Daire. I might have to bite you several times."

The thought of her sinking her fangs into me—while my dick was turning purple beneath the ropes—made me squirm and arch beneath her. I would have thrown myself against her without Rik's heavy palm pressing me down.

With agonizing slowness, they unwound the tight loops from around my wrists and arms. My fingers tingled and ached. Ever so gently, she pulled the rope away from my tortured flesh. My eyes burned and I hissed out a long breath. Fuuuuuck. All the sensation poured through me. Burning, blazing blood. So much need.

Still. Even after Guillaume had used me.

Shame burned my cheeks in a hot flash. Her other Blood should have all taken a turn too. Maybe that would slake this need to be used and abused so she wouldn't have to.

She scraped her fang over the edge of my ear. "Oh, but I want to, D. Very much indeed."

SHARA

Hearing the soft, fragile sounds escaping his mouth woke something in me. Something ravenous and brutal.

All my rage came boiling back up inside me.

The horror of seeing the woman who'd raised me turned into a walking corpse. The impotent rage standing before Marne, bound by my word and Aima law. Even when she hurt my Blood.

I saw the spear protruding from Rik's shoulder again and wildfire swept through me.

Daire let out a muffled groan, his face shoved down against the mattress by Rik. "Take it out on me, my queen. Make me hurt. Make me bleed. I don't care. I want it all."

I climbed on top of him, straddling his thighs, my hands braced on either side of his ribcage. "Rik's going to fuck me now and see how many times he can make me claw your back. How does that sound?"

"Fucking perfect," they both said at the same time.

Rik dropped down against my back, giving me his weight. Smashing me down against Daire so I was pressed tightly between two layers of sheer muscle. "Let it all out, Shara."

I rested my forehead against Daire's back, breathing in his warm scent of musk and fur. Soaking in Rik's unshakeable strength, I let the image of Mom's corpse fill my head again. The rotting, gray flesh. The tattered lapis-blue dress. Her eyes, huge and shining with sheer terror. Fully aware of the rotting creature her soul was trapped inside.

Shuddering, I clamped my hands around Daire's shoulders and dug in my long, sharp nails. They pierced him easily. Spicy and feral, his blood flowed into me. With a sensual stroke of fur winding through our bonds, his warcat let out an earth-shaking roar. Pleasure, yes, but also with rage.

My rage.

Bubbling up out of me like a volcano.

I raked his back with both hands. Thumped my fists against the steel planes of muscle beneath me. I stabbed him with my nails. Ripped him again.

Marne fucking Ceresa's face filled my head. Her smug arrogant smile. Her power lashing me, trying to drive me to my knees, or better yet, to break my word and violate our agreement.

"Fucking bitch. I hate her! I hate them both!"

Daire's purr roared up out of him, vibrating his entire body against me. Rik clamped his hands on my hips and adjusted me so I could rub my clit on Daire's thigh. I ground against him, torturing him with the wet, hot glide of my bare pussy on his skin. Flattening his tongue against my throat, Rik licked a lazy path from my ear down to the vein pounding just beneath the surface.

Everything inside me winched tighter with anticipation. I wanted his fangs. I wanted his dick. I wanted his blood.

I wanted it all.

Rearing back, he thrust deeply into me on a long, hard glide that made me drag my nails down Daire's back again. Rik slammed up inside me and I shoved my nails deeper. Again. The scent of blood made me light-headed with hunger, even though I was already feeding thanks to my vampire nails.

I wanted—needed—so much more.

I sank my fangs into the meaty part of Daire's shoulder. His back bowed up beneath me, his arms flailing frantically. His hips jerked, forcing me up harder against Rik. Keeping my fangs in Daire's shoulder, I held him inside my mouth. Tasting him. Feeling him inside me. While Rik drove us both higher.

When he finally bit my throat, I screamed around my mouthful of Daire. I clawed at his back, drinking him down while Rik feasted at my throat. I came again, harder, my heart trying to pound out of my ribcage. Daire's blood coated my face. My breasts. I didn't try to heal him yet. His blood felt too good, tingling and burning as it soaked into my skin.

Panting, Rik slid out of me and dropped down to lie beside Daire. But I wasn't finished. I rolled over on top of Daire and wiggled around on his back. Smearing his blood on me. Wallowing on him. Reveling in his blood until I looked like the victim of a murder scene.

Lying on top of him, I stared up at the ceiling. My chest heaved with exertion and my eyes burned. My throat ached. But the heavy weight that had been crushing my chest was gone.

I hadn't even realized it was there, until now I felt its absence. I couldn't believe how much better I felt. Lighter. More myself.

Closing my eyes, I swept my power through Daire, wiping away the injuries I'd given him. I winced. I'd done quite a number on his back but he didn't seem to mind. In fact, he only purred louder, giving me a little bump by thrusting his butt up beneath me.

"I'll never mind anything you do to me. I mean it. Besides, I needed it more than you did."

I slid off to his side so I could lie between them. My original vampire knights. I tried to remember the scared girl I'd been when they found me. Fighting off monsters with a pocket knife and a bucket of salt. It seemed ages ago, even though it'd actually only been a few months.

Daire nestled his face against my breasts. "Next time, throw some fucking salt on Marne Ceresa. If nothing else, it'll make her soup taste better, right?"

I wrapped my arms around his head, curling myself around him, with Rik hot and solid against my back. Softly, I whispered, "Could I have done anything differently?"

Rik dropped his chin against my shoulder. "No."

He said it without hesitation, that single word echoing with assurance and confidence.

"But you're worried about another attack from the Dauphine. Maybe I should have struck against her myself. Gone to New Orleans. Something... more. I don't know what Marne will actually do to her."

His arms tightened around me. "No. I'm not worried. Why do you say that?"

I turned around enough in his arms to see his face. "You gave specific orders for the guard and mentioned her attacking us again."

"But that's not worry. That's just being smart. She may attack the nest again, but you were prepared last time too. Your trees had her messenger trapped before you arrived. Your warning system activated immediately. Unless she can manage to send hundreds of those zombies against the nest, I don't think anything would ever penetrate deeply enough to actually threaten you. Even then, you'd just burn them up."

Daire peeked up at me, his molten eyes shining with heat and love. "Because you're Shara fucking Isador, Triskeles queen of America."

The last bit of my self-doubt crumbled away. Pressed between my Blood, I closed my eyes. Muscle by muscle, I relaxed, releasing the last bit of tension that lingered. Daire's rumbling purr rocked me deeper toward sleep.

I listened a moment, trying to find the queen trapped in darkness. Was she safe yet? Had she called her Blood? How would I know?

I could probably go to the tower in New York City and use the darkness in the basement to find out, but I didn't feel like budging. Not now. Maybe not for days. Weeks.

"Sounds good to me." Rik kissed my shoulder. "But we could always build you a place of darkness here so you don't have to travel. In fact... remember the grotto?"

I was already too sleepy to answer him. I'd wished for a place like Mayte's grotto, and when we'd returned from Mexico, it was here. Exactly like I'd imagined.

Sinking deeper into sleep, I built my ideal place of darkness in my mind.

I walked down curving steps, trailing my fingers along

the cold, stone wall. A spiral staircase, carved from layers of rock. But it wasn't claustrophobic or tight. I could feel open air on my skin. As I neared the bottom of the staircase, deep purple flows of shadow inched up my legs. My waist. My neck. Until with the last step, I sank completely beneath the pooled darkness of my father's legacy to me.

Welcome home, Daughter.

2

QUEEN TAKES ALPHA

For Kimberly
(Takes place after Queen Takes Queen but before Skye Tower falls
in Queen Takes Rook)

SHARA

Rik gave me a smoldering look that made my fangs ache. "How would you like us tonight, my queen?"

I didn't answer right away, allowing my gaze to touch each of my Blood. Each man was a magnificent warrior and protector, eager to fulfill my every fantasy. Mehen's emerald eyes glittered, locked to my every move, very much the mighty Leviathan. My warcat's purr rumbled like deep thunder, making my bones vibrate even though Daire wasn't touching me. Yet.

Xin didn't say a word or move a muscle, but his wolf poised inside him, ready to pounce.

My twins. My Templar knight. My burly bear. My dark raven.

How could I possibly choose?

"I have an idea," Mehen said in a silky voice of menace that managed to carry a hint of his dragon's hiss. "Let Rik choose. Let him be alpha."

"He is alpha," I replied slowly, not sure what point he was trying to make. "Always."

Rik cupped my cheek in his palm and gently tilted my face up to his. "He means let me dictate who and how tonight."

His warm palm was so big. So strong. If he chose, he could palm my head like a basketball, or smash me like a melon. Yet when he touched me, he was unfailingly gentle.

Images flickered through my head. Of Rik *not* being gentle.

Demanding. Dominant. Possessive. Dangerous.

Alpha.

Like when he'd put Mehen in a choke-hold and fucked him into submission.

Rik had never handled me like that. Ever.

We'd fucked countless times in multiple combinations with my other Blood. Even another woman. But he'd never *taken* me.

He bent down and brushed his lips against mine, his words a caress that made my eyes flutter shut. "You're my queen. I love you more than life itself. I will give you anything you desire, my queen. Gladly. We all will."

"Aye, "yes," "my queen..." Echoed around the room as my Blood agreed with him.

I wrapped my arms around Rik's neck and stared up into his eyes so I could watch his reaction. "Tonight, I want my alpha to take me any way *he* desires."

His eyes blazed. He slid his palm through my hair and

cupped my nape, squeezing just enough to make my eyes flare. "Are you sure that's what you want, my queen?"

He hadn't even touched me sexually yet, but my body was primed. Everything throbbed in time with my heartbeat. My fangs. My clit. I licked my lips and nodded. "Without question."

His fingers tightened on my neck, sending my pulse into overdrive. Already, he seemed bigger, meaner, as if his rock troll was swelling beneath his skin. "G, use your knives to cut our queen's clothes off her body."

Guillaume stepped closer, already pulling a slender silver blade out of one of his wrist sheathes. "Gladly, alpha."

My breathing quickened. I didn't know why. I wasn't afraid. Not of Guillaume, and certainly not of Rik. My Templar knight's loyalty and honor were above reproach. He'd even cut my clothes off before.

So, what made this different?

Maybe it was the way Rik kept me locked into place, his fingers gripping me so hard that he could have picked me up off the floor and held me dangling like a kitten in his grip. Or maybe it was knowing that my other Blood watched. All of them. I could feel their attention locked on me as Guillaume took my hand in his.

His thumb dug into my palm and ground against my tendons, making my breath catch in my throat. He jerked a little as he straightened my arm out to the side, almost too far. Enough that I could feel the pull in my inner elbow and a bit of strain in my wrist. Nothing to hurt me...

But a deliberate reminder.

Each of my Blood were strong, powerful men. Men who could grab me, bend me to their will, and use their strength against me, unless I called on my power to protect myself. They would never threaten me like that, though. They *chose* to submit to me as their queen. They kept their fierce predators under control when they touched me.

Unless I wished for them to be unleashed.

The cold silver blade touched my inner wrist. Guillaume paused, waiting for me to meet his gaze. "Slow?" He kept his voice soft, even though his eyes glinted like the steel blade in his hand. "Or fast?"

I started to open my mouth, but Rik clamped his fingers harder on my neck. Whatever I'd been about to say scattered like fallen leaves in a hurricane.

"Slow." Rik's graveled voice made goosebumps race down my arm. "Until I say otherwise."

"Understood, alpha."

The knife edged up my wrist and the delicate fibers of my sweater leapt apart beneath the razor-sharp edge. Guillaume had no problem slicing through the fibers, though every once in a while, he paused and gave another little tug on my arm, turning my wrist slightly to keep the strain on my muscles. To remind me that he held me. That he controlled the position of my arm, while Rik controlled... everything else.

"Mehen," he growled out Leviathan's true name like a curse. "Strip. Flat on your back on the bed."

I half expected Mehen to bitch, or at least send a dirty glare Rik's way, but he jerked his shirt off and shucked his pants without a word. He stretched out on my bed as ordered, only he chose to lay sideways, rather than putting his head on the pillows. He scooted closer to the edge and pushed his head back, tipping his chin up and allowing his head to sag off the mattress, so he could still watch as Guillaume made his way up my shoulder.

"Daire," Rik said, stalling my warcat's purr momentarily. "Ready the dragon for our queen."

Flashing a grin, Daire undressed so quickly that I almost missed it. He pounced on the bed and jarred Mehen enough that the dragon muttered a curse, only because he lost sight of me. Daire dropped to his belly and rubbed against the other man's legs, wriggling playfully up Mehen's thighs.

I found myself holding my breath. Waiting. Watching as Daire pretended like he didn't see the massive dick begging for his attention. He purred and rubbed against Mehen's legs until the dragon reached down, seized a handful of his hair, and dragged him exactly where he wanted Daire to be.

"Oh." Daire bumped his dick with his chin but deliberately avoided the man's efforts of hauling his mouth into place. "I don't think he needs any help, Rik. He's pretty fucking ready for our queen already."

"But she's not," Rik replied.

Oh, but I was. I could feel how wet I was. If Rik and Guillaume didn't keep me locked in place, I would have already joined my two Blood in bed.

Guillaume sliced up through the top of my sweater. Cold steel eased up my throat, drawing my attention to him.

"Do the next sleeve quickly," Rik growled.

Guillaume's lips quirked. He grabbed my other arm, pulled it straight, as he'd done before, and paused a moment with the knife at my wrist. "Don't move, my queen. I'd regret drawing a single drop of your sweet blood without our alpha's permission."

I held my breath, anticipating rising.

A low groan from Mehen told me Daire had finally quit teasing him. I glanced over and locked eyes with Daire as he came up for air and smacked his lips. "He tastes good, my queen. But not as good as you."

His hair was tousled around his shoulders like a wild, shaggy mane. His eyes gleamed like his warcat on the prowl. He sank down over Mehen's dick again, holding my gaze, forcing the erect cock so deeply into his throat that I couldn't understand how he wasn't choking.

"Shara." Guillaume whispered my name like a prayer, jerking my attention to him. Then he zipped the knife up my sleeve so fast I couldn't help but gasp. The sound of tearing fabric was surprisingly loud and awful. My heart pounded as my sweater seemed to dissolve off my body in an instant, held only by the intact neckband around my throat.

"Very good," Rik said, a dark edge in his voice that I'd never heard. "It's almost like skinning a deer. Do her jeans now, but leave the band around her throat, in case our queen gets cold."

With a grin, Guillaume tucked the slender blade back up his sleeve and reached over his shoulder. Oh no. I knew what that meant.

He was getting the biggest knife that he carried in a spine sheath.

The heavy knife was at least a foot long. How he wore that thing hidden down his back, and drew it without nicking himself, I had no idea. I didn't care about the knife, though. Not with Daire's head bobbing so enthusiastically on Mehen's cock. My dragon had one hand fisted in Daire's hair, and his other wrapped in the bedding, muscles and tendons standing in stark relief.

Though his glittering emerald eyes were still locked on me, despite my other Blood's mouth on his dick. His eyes blazed. He wanted to seize me and drag me beneath him. He wanted to slam into me so hard that we broke the bed or brought the walls tumbling down around us.

However, he did absolutely nothing at all but lie there and allow Daire to tease him. Because my alpha hadn't given him permission.

Yet.

Guillaume gathered the hem of my jeans in his left hand and set the tip inside my pants leg, ready to cut through the thick ankle hem, but he paused. "These jeans do look very nice on you, my queen. They fit you so well that we all jostle for the right to walk behind you, so we can drool over the way they hug your ass and thighs so perfectly. Maybe you would rather I not cut them apart?"

I swallowed, trying to get my brain to work.

"Cut them off," Rik ordered. "Our queen has other jeans that fit as well, and if not, we'll buy them for her. We'll buy so many that you can cut them off her every single night."

"I'd like that." Guillaume winked at me and set to work cutting the thick denim. Each tug and rip made me want to jerk frantically at the button and shimmy out of my jeans and be done. But Rik wanted this, and so did Guillaume. All I had to do was stand here and let him slide that huge blade up the inside of my thigh, cutting as meticulously as the finest surgeon.

While my dragon moaned and tossed his head, driven mad by Daire's talented tongue.

I was practically dancing in place myself as Guillaume made his way up my other thigh. He pulled the waistband away from my stomach and shielded my tender skin with his fingers as he sawed up through the thicker band. I ran my hands over his head, stroking his cheeks and combing my fingers through his curls. His hair was dark and full, now. Unlike when he'd first come to me, almost dead from starvation. His hands and fingers had been broken and misshapen from torture, his hair and face gray with exhaustion and weakness.

The last Templar knight. Now whole, hearty, and hale, on his knees, cutting my pants off.

He kissed my stomach as my jeans fell away, but then rose to his feet and gave Rik a salute. "Task accomplished, alpha."

Rik slid his fingers beneath the tattered neckband of my sweater. "Are you cold?"

I shook my head. "Not at all."

He tore through the remaining band holding my sweater to my body and tossed the material aside. Still gripping my nape, he swung me up against him and carried me toward the bed. His skin was so hot against mine. When had he stripped his clothes off? I couldn't remember. I wanted more. So much more. His weight smashing me into the mattress. His big, powerful body moving on top of me. Inside me. Driving me higher. My fangs throbbed, but I resisted the urge to bite him.

If I bit him, he'd be done for a while. My bite carried an orgasmic punch that I didn't want to waste so quickly. My alpha always recovered quickly, unless he'd tasted the cream between my thighs. Then he'd been known to pass out because he came so hard.

He set me down on top of Mehen's chest. My dragon immediately seized my hips, but Rik stalled him from dragging me down his body.

"Not yet." Rik laughed, a wicked edge to his voice that made Mehen grind his teeth. "You're her appetizer. You're going to get me ready for our queen while she takes her pleasure in you."

My eyes widened, and I braced for a surge of fury or denial from Mehen. He could be an arrogant bastard at his best. While he'd allowed Rik to fuck him when he first joined me as Blood, he'd been desperate. Who wouldn't have been after thousands of years locked away in a prison with only rats and the occasional foolish queen who thought to free him as a snack?

"Bring it the fuck on, alpha." He tipped his head up enough to look up at me with a fierce, smiling snarl on his lips. "I'll do anything to get a taste of our queen. Anything at all."

Then he dropped his head back down over the side of the

mattress and opened his mouth. Waiting for Rik to fuck his throat.

I watched, unable to look away, even if Marne Ceresa herself tried to blast me off the face of this earth. Rik leaned down over the other man's body, bracing one hand on the mattress while he guided his dick with the other. He pushed into Mehen's mouth and let out a pleased grunt that sounded like distant thunder.

"Daire, help our queen give the dragon his reward."

Daire grabbed me around the waist and dragged me backward over Mehen's groin. "He's nice and hard for you, my queen. Though he'll probably come too quickly to satisfy you."

:Like hell I will,: Mehen retorted in our bonds, since his mouth was full.

I loved having one of my Blood's impressive erections sliding into me. Always. But tonight, he seemed sharper, harder, thicker, longer. Impossibly so. I shivered and moaned softly as I took his cock inside me. I actually had to pause a moment, bracing my hands on his stomach to catch my breath.

Or maybe I just wanted my full concentration on how Rik was fucking his mouth. Rik moved slowly, but there wasn't anything hesitant about the way he glided deeper into the other man's throat. His body moved in a slow, steady thrust, the veins standing out in stark relief in his neck and shoulders, but he had no trouble controlling himself. In fact, he looked up at me with heavy-lidded eyes and a lazy smile.

"Do you like what you see, my queen?"

I gulped and nodded vigorously. Very much. They were putting this show on for my full benefit. Enjoying each other —for my pleasure. I'd never really thought about it before in quite this way. If given a choice, I'm sure they'd each rather be inside me, than one of their brethren, but if given the opportunity to please me, even by fucking another man, they were eager. Ready. And more than willing.

Shuddering, I finally seated Mehen fully inside me. He gripped my thighs and shifted beneath me, planting his feet on the mattress so he could rock up into me. Daire pressed against my back, squeezing in between Mehen's knees. My fangs ached so badly that I couldn't close my mouth, which had the unfortunate side effect of making me drool all over Mehen's stomach. Not that he cared.

I watched the long muscles of his throat working on Rik's cock. He literally swallowed Rik down, making my alpha rumble with pleasure. Though Rik controlled the pace—and not just for himself. Every time Rik thrust deeper, Mehen rocked up into me.

Rik was fucking me—and he wasn't even touching me.

Sweat glistened on Mehen's chest. His abdominal muscles quivered beneath my hands. I dug my fingers in harder, reveling in the feel of sheer muscle moving beneath my palms.

:Please,: he growled in our bond, making even his plea sound like a demand. *:Bite me when I come.:*

Rik leaned forward even more so he could kiss me. I felt the flex of his mighty body, thrusting deeply into my other Blood, and climax suddenly broke through me. I hadn't realized I was so close. I gasped, my back arching. Thankfully that pulled me away from Rik, so I punctured my own lips and not his, which would have pushed him over the edge too soon. My blood splattered on Mehen's stomach and he pitched beneath me.

:Fuck, Shara, please!:

I leaned down and sank my fangs into Mehen's pectoral muscle directly over his heart. He shoved up into me, his spine bowing hard. Rik grunted and muttered a curse. Distantly, I wondered if Mehen had bitten him accidentally.

Power crested inside me, fed by my blood and the surge of pleasure pouring through my body. I tried to send healing energy Rik's way, just in case, but I couldn't concentrate.

Not with Mehen's blood sliding down my throat.

All my Blood tasted incredible and Mehen was no different, though his blood always carried a bit of a razor's edge that my other Blood didn't possess. He was the only one who would have killed me, if I hadn't managed to outwit him and bring him to heel. Leviathan would have gleefully drained me dry and reveled in my alpha's misery. He would have used my death to free himself from his prison in a heartbeat.

:My freedom without you would have been a worse prison than the millennia I'd already spent locked away alone.: He panted in our bond, plumes of smoke from his dragon. *:Even with your alpha's dick shoved down my throat.:*

Choking back teary laugher, I licked my puncture marks closed and raised my head. My hunger roiled inside me, but I didn't want him to pass out. Not if Rik had further plans for him.

"I definitely do," Rik said. "Ezra, it's time for you to help Daire entertain our queen."

"Fucking A." The mattress dipped behind me, and I heard a playful slap. By the way Daire purred, that'd been his ass getting smacked.

Rik closed his hands around my waist and started to lift me, but Mehen clutched my thighs for dear life, even though his mouth was still stuffed. *:Not yet, alpha. Wouldn't it give her more pleasure if we were both inside her?:*

"The lizard has a point," Ezra said. "If you turn her around, I'll set Daire to work bringing him back to full staff and keep her revved up too."

It was amazing how quickly four sets of male hands could turn me around, and though Mehen had climaxed once already, he was sizeable enough—and certainly interested enough in round two—that his dick didn't slide out of me. Facing his feet, rather than his head, made for a much different angle inside me. I started to lean forward to brace my palms on his thighs, but Rik wrapped his forearm around my throat and pulled me back against his broad chest.

It took me a minute to realize he must have come up on top of Mehen too. By the way his palms glided all over me, I didn't think he minded in the slightest.

"Hardly," Mehen laughed as he slipped his fingers deeper between my thighs. He even managed to twist around enough to get his mouth on my arm. "I'll gladly be on the bottom of this pile any night."

Daire dipped down and stroked his tongue over my pelvic bone from one hip to the other. He made a leisurely trip down to my pussy, flicking his tongue over my flesh and Mehen's fingers at the same time. Rik tightened his forearm around my throat, deliberately arching me backwards so Daire had more access.

That wicked tongue. Goddess. Daire had licked me plenty of times and I always loved it. But knowing that Mehen was enjoying it too, took it to a whole new level. My dragon chuckled and tipped his hips, pushing inside me as deeply as he could. "Definitely a very nice bonus."

Ezra crawled closer and slid up behind Daire's buttocks. "Lick her real good and that dick inside her too, while I work your ass over."

Daire locked his lips around my clit and let his purr roll through my body. My muscles twitched, and I groaned. I couldn't stay still, even with Rik pinning me against him. Ezra tore his wrist open and bled down Daire's back and buttocks. My nostrils flared, catching the scent of pine and cinnamon. I swallowed and pitched harder against Rik, but he didn't loosen his grip on my throat.

"Yeah, sweetheart," Ezra crooned softly as he eased into Daire. "Tell us how much you want us."

Rik rumbled against my ear. "I'll make him do as you say, my queen. Anything you want. It's yours. As your alpha, I can do no less."

"I want his blood," I rasped out. "I want his hook in Daire. I want you inside me, Rik. Please. And then I want more blood. I want everyone's blood."

"You heard our queen."

Ezra planted his elbow on Daire's shoulders to keep his head down and out of his way, so he could lean closer and press his bleeding wrist to my mouth. I tried to keep my eyes open, so I could watch the way he moved inside Daire, but the taste of his blood swept me to a distant mountain cabin. A fire crackled in the fireplace that smelled of smoldering cinnamon. Snow whispered in the pine trees against the window. Thick fur tickling my nose. My bear.

Through our bonds, I felt him shove deep inside of Daire and release the mating hook. Daire writhed against me, but he refused to lift his mouth. I remembered all too well what the sudden expansion of that hook felt like. The incredible sense of fullness that was almost too much. Almost pain. But oh, so fucking good.

The scent of smoking hot rock and iron made my mouth water. Rik's blood. I would have released Ezra's wrist to take Rik's blood instead, but my bear pushed harder against my mouth.

"More, sweetheart. Take me down to the last drop."

Blood dripped on my shoulders and down my back. Each drop like a sizzling trail of molten wax. "This blood has another purpose for now."

Mehen's erection swelled inside me, his anticipation growing. Rik tipped me forward, letting his blood drip down my buttocks. Daire kept his face buried in my pussy, even though I was almost doubled over him. I wasn't sure how he was going to breathe, but I couldn't care as Rik started to slide into me. I was too busy trying to breathe myself.

None of my Blood were small men. Though Mehen wasn't as big as Guillaume, who claimed the title of "hung like a hell horse," it was still delicious agony to have them both inside me at the same time. I could feel their dicks gliding through me. Almost touching. So deep. I couldn't. I wanted. No words.

:You don't need words,: Rik whispered in my head, targeting only my bond. Only my alpha had the power to speak privately into my mind. *:Never for me.:*

My Blood came to me. All of them. Touching me. Their blood...

It was too much. My power surged, surely too high. I couldn't contain it all. It would burn me out and destroy us all, but I couldn't hold back. Power and pleasure both spilled into my Bloods' bonds, lighting up the threads that tied us together in my mind. So bright. I couldn't see my men any longer. I couldn't see anything but the blistering heat rising inside me.

But I felt them. I smelled them. I tasted them. Nevarre's hair and ancient Celtic magic. The elegant swipe of blue-green feathers in a sinuous glide through my mind. Roasted coffee and chocolate, the quiet whine of a dog. The ice-cold touch of my silent wolf that burned like quicksilver. Sulfur and brimstone, a stallion's whicker. My warcat's continuous purr that vibrated through my bones. A hissing puff of smoke. A grouchy growl from a grizzly.

The heavy, massive weight of a rock troll against my back.

I climaxed, endlessly, the rise and fall of a symphony that carried me into darkness. I didn't know how long I faded out. It could have been minutes. Or hours. Weeks. I felt like

Rip Van Winkle, only instead of sleeping, I'd been coming for a hundred years.

Blood and come burned on my skin, feeding my power. I could feel my body soaking it up like a sponge, turning their offerings into magic that I would use to obliterate our enemies, as effortlessly as they'd just obliterated me.

I lay on an impressive mountain of muscles. Tangled limbs and powerful hands and sheer rock-hard muscle, touching me everywhere, though it was Rik's heartbeat beneath my cheek. I lifted my head and he shoved the heavy fall of hair out of my eyes so I could see him. His lips curved in a supremely smug smile that he completely deserved.

"Wow," I finally managed to say.

"Did your alpha live up to your expectations, my queen?"

Maybe my brain still wasn't working. I couldn't seem to organize my thoughts.

I'd asked him to take me, anyway that he wanted. Which he'd done, yes, but somehow...

I'd still been in control, even when I'd given that control to him.

His thumb feathered over my lips. "Of course. You're my queen."

"But..."

He leaned up and licked the corner of my mouth, finding some blood that I'd missed. He rumbled, so softly, my mighty yet gentle giant. "My queen takes what she wants, even when she asks to be taken."

I curled my arms around his neck and I pressed my mouth more fully to his. *:Consider yourself taken, alpha.:*

3

QUEEN TAKES TWINS

(Written after Queen Takes Checkmate – set at a future Halloween)

TLACEL

"I've never been in a place long enough to decorate for a holiday," Shara said. "Let alone Halloween. We won't have trick-or-treaters so far out at the manor house, will we?"

Rik had sent my brother and I ahead to act as point guards, while he and Daire walked on either side of her down the sidewalk. The rest of her Blood formed a loose arc of protection as she window-shopped. Not that our queen feared much these days.

After a harrowing journey to Egypt, our queen had enjoyed several quiet months at home in her nest. Eureka Springs, Arkansas might be a strange place for a powerful vampire queen to call home, but her nest had become a

magical place that welcomed her. From the grove of impossibly ancient trees that encircled her home, to the bubbling
hot spring large enough to accommodate as many Blood as
she cared to call, the nest changed the very terrain of the
earth to please her.

We each would do anything to make her smile.

We walked down a steep street lined with small, unique
shops decorated with pumpkins, straw bales, and wreaths of
Indian corn and leaves. Eureka Springs had been carved out
of the treacherous cracks between the Ozark mountains,
with buildings practically stacked on top of each other. Many
were built deeply into the grottos and hollows in the steep
cliffs. Though the title of "historic" Eureka Springs made
most of us Blood shake our heads with amusement. Itztli and
I had been born long before this area had ever been popu-
lated, and we weren't even the eldest Blood.

Our queen drew some curious glances from the humans
wandering the streets. We were all dressed in jeans and T-
shirts, even our queen, but they must have thought she was a
celebrity with so many bodyguards. Itztli gave a long, hard
look at a man walking up the sidewalk toward us. He blinked
and immediately crossed the street, watching warily over his
shoulder to be sure we weren't coming after him.

"If you want trick-or-treaters to come out to the manor,
we could have a Halloween party and invite the whole city,"
Daire said. "You wouldn't even need to decorate much. Just
have us all shifted and roaming the grounds. It'd scare the
shit out of everybody."

Mehen let out a disgusted grunt. "Human children are
bloody annoying, and they don't even make a very good
mouthful."

Shara laughed. "Since you can't go around eating children, I suppose there won't be any Halloween party at the
manor."

I touched my twin's bond. *:Do you think we could find some calaveras? We could celebrate Día de Muertos instead. Or Mayte could send a sib to us with supplies.:*

:I think our queen would appreciate the chance to celebrate the lives of her ancestors,: Itztli replied. *:I saw some sugar skulls a few shops back on the opposite side.:*

I lightly touched Rik's bond. *:Alpha...:*

:Go,: Rik said immediately, showing us exactly how entangled our Blood bonds were with one another. *:Find what you need, and meet us back at the car in an hour.:*

Itztli and I immediately crossed the street and headed back up the hill. I heard Shara ask, "Where are they going?"

Rik tucked her arm around his and led her to the next shop. "They want to put together a surprise for you."

Our queen had enough power to blast the sun god to the underworld and drain the queen of New York City to her death, but she didn't demand answers from us. She wouldn't want to spoil our surprise.

Which was only one of the many reasons we loved her more than life itself.

SHARA

It took a surprising amount of determination to ignore my twins' bonds and allow them to keep their secrets. I was always aware of my Blood, even when they were quieter and more reserved. Even Xin, who could be invisible from everyone but me, was a constant, tangible weight in my mind. At a moment's notice, I could touch his bond and sense his ghostly wolf prowling the nest.

Itztli and Tlacel were two of the quieter Blood. Though they'd been with me since the New Year, I still didn't know them as deeply as my other Blood. Rik and Daire had been with me from the beginning. They were always by my side, especially my alpha. Guillaume and Mehen, as the oldest, were nearby and ready for me to consult them on a tricky Triune situation or another house. Ezra and Vivian were too belligerent to ever be overlooked or forgotten.

Llewellyn was almost as old as Guillaume and had the benefit of knowing my mother before her death. Naturally, I spent a great deal of time with him, asking about his memories of Esetta Isador, the queen who'd sacrificed everything, including her life and her Blood, to have me.

Nevarre was another quiet Blood, but I depended on him heavily to guard from the sky. He'd also called the crow queen to my nest, and now hundreds of birds came and went from my trees, carrying secrets and stolen gifts from all over the world to share their knowledge with us.

But the twins didn't feel as if they'd made a significant contribution to me yet, though I completely disagreed. Itztli had sacrificed himself to help me grow the heart tree for his sister's nest. Tlacel had been instrumental in helping me understand Huitzilopochtli when I'd first awakened him. Plus, I just loved them. I loved Itztli's incredible sense of smell when he shifted into his black dog. His absolute trust in me, even when he wanted and needed me to hurt him. He'd seen me kill before, and yet came to me willingly, depending on me to fulfill his darker needs.

Tlacel always reminded me of the lush jungle, and he'd been the one to pull me back from the portal when we'd almost lost his niece, Xochitl. I'd be dead without them. So how could they doubt my love for them?

"They don't doubt you or your love," Rik said, his voice a low, rumbling landslide of boulders. "They saw an opportunity to do something unique for you, and they wish to make you smile. That's all."

Halloween came and went without any surprise, so I

wasn't sure what they might be planning. And no, we didn't have a single trick-or-treater, much to Mehen's disappointment.

At dusk on November 1st, I came down for dinner to find all the lights off downstairs. Candles formed a glowing path toward the back of the house. A fire burned in the fireplace, but it didn't smell like normal wood. Something spicy and fragrant filled the air. Dozens of candles gleamed on the mantel, tables, and shelves all around the room.

Rik let go of my hand and stepped back, leaving me in the center of the room. Though I wasn't alone. I could feel my Blood all around me, even in the darkness.

Itztli stepped out of the shadows by the fireplace. His face was painted bone white with dark circles around his eyes and mouth, giving him a ghoulish look. Though as he came closer, I could see bright flowers painted on his forehead and cheeks. Tlacel approached from the other side of the room, drawing my attention to him. He'd painted his face, too. They were both naked, their chests streaked with white and black paint that resembled bones.

"Today's the first day of Día de Muertos," Itztli said. "The Day of the Dead. We have prepared an altar for your ancestors, if you'd like to see it."

I took his hand and he drew me over to a table beneath the window. Candles gleamed on the polished wood, illuminating vases of golden flowers. Sugar skulls painted with brilliant splashes of color were mixed in with the flowers. Hanging on the wall was an ornate oval picture frame that stole my breath.

My mother. Esetta Isador.

She'd died at my birth and I'd never seen a picture of her, but I looked so much like her that I would know her image anywhere. Her long dark hair was piled on her head with curls hanging down around her cheeks. Her eyes glittered like dark sapphires on midnight velvet. Isis's crown sat on her head.

But it was the smile on her face that made my eyes fill with tears. It was like she looked out of the picture and smiled with love. For me and me alone.

"Where did you find this?" I whispered, fighting back tears.

"I painted it," Itztli replied.

Startled, I searched his face. "But how? Did you know her?"

He took my hand and kissed my knuckles. "I know her only through you, my queen, though Llewellyn shared images of her through our bond."

"It's a very good likeness," Llewellyn said from the edge of the room, though he didn't come any closer.

I felt like there was more to see, but it was hard to drag my gaze away from hers. Another portrait sat in a simple frame on the table. This one was more abstract with bold, heavy strokes of darkness and fire. Shadows pooled around the bottom of the painting, but I could make out snake heads and glittering red eyes. A man's bare chest rose out of the darkness with harsh, regal features.

Typhon, father of monsters. My father.

"He was harder to paint, since no one has seen him but you, my queen," Tlacel said. "I hope it's a good likeness. I didn't want to pry too deeply into your mind without your permission."

"It's gorgeous. I had no idea you both knew how to paint. Would you paint each of my Blood too, including each other?"

Itztli bowed over my hand and kissed my knuckles again. "It would be an honor, my queen."

"What else is on the altar?"

Tlacel explained each item. "We bake this special bread

called pan de muerto. Mayte was glad to send some up from Zaniyah, along with some of our traditional foods. Mole, tamales, and whatever foods the deceased enjoyed. Winston will also serve your mother's favorite seafood for dinner tonight. The yellow flowers are cempoalxochitl, or Aztec marigolds. We often plant them in cemeteries and their petals are used to mark the pathway to the deceased's altar."

I touched Mayte's bond and silently said, :*thank you*.: "Xochitl? Did her name come from the marigolds?"

"Cempoalxochitl means twenty flower, because of its many petals," Itztli replied. "When his daughter was born, Tepeyollotl declared her as beautiful as a flower, and so her name was decided."

"It's beautiful," I whispered as I slipped an arm around each man's waist to draw them closer. They hugged me between them, smearing my sweater with paint, but I didn't mind. "Thank you. Thank you for sharing your heritage with me."

"Always," Itztli said, while Tlacel added, "Our pleasure."

I slipped my hand up Itztli's back, enjoying the play of muscle beneath my fingers. He was built more solidly and thickly than his brother. "Will you share something else with me?"

"Without question."

Tipping my head back so I could look into his eyes, I waited until he bent down to me, offering his throat. I fluttered my lips across his skin, breathing in his scent. Spicy cocoa laced with cayenne pepper. His blood called to me. "Would it be disrespectful to your traditions if I fucked you and Tlacel while you feed me?"

A low, rumbling chuckle escaped from his throat. "Why else would we come to you naked, my queen?"

ITZTLI

Anticipation coiled in my stomach, a live hot wire of tension. But this night wasn't about me.

Shara understood my needs and had already helped fulfill that dark hunger several times. She didn't mind that I was descended from the Flayed God, who reveled in pain and blood. From the beginning, she hadn't flinched away. She'd used my obsidian blade to sacrifice me, pulling my still-beating heart from my chest, only to give it back, along with all her love.

Tlacel hadn't yet embraced his full need.

His bond was drawn up tight inside my head, a shivering knot of worry and fear. He didn't fear our queen, not at all. He feared that she would find him lacking. That his need... would somehow disqualify him as her Blood. That she would carve him out of her life as easily as she'd cut my heart from my chest.

He didn't yet understand the depths to which our queen cared for us. Not fully. But he had me to help him.

"My queen," I whispered. "May we make a request?"

She lifted her head and met my gaze at once. "Of course."

"My brother has a need that remains unfulfilled."

Turning to him, she cupped his face in both her palms. "Tlacel? What is it? What's wrong?" Because he was trembling.

She didn't move, but her bond overflowed with sweet, crystal waters glittering with the light of a full moon. Her power rose, filling my nose with the scents of a desert. Blowing sands, night blooming jasmine, and the rich, dark scent of loam found deep in the forest, untouched by the sun. She flowed through us both, reading our secrets and my brother's unspoken need.

Stroking his cheeks, she slid her hands up past his ears

and tangled her fingers in his hair. She tightened her grip slowly, watching his face. Reading his bond. His eyes tightened with the subtle pain, but that wasn't why she did it. Tlacel didn't enjoy pain like me.

She moved her fingers to his nape, her head tilting slightly as she listened to his bond. Squeezing her fingers on his neck, she felt the moment he relaxed into her grip. "Ah," she breathed out, her lips curving into a soft, knowing smile. "Itztli, would you have something handy that we can use to tie your brother up?"

Tlacel's eyes flared wide with shock. Not at her suggestion—but at her easy acceptance of his need. He didn't want pain. He wanted to be bound. He wanted to be made helpless.

For our queen and she alone.

"Of course, my queen."

SHARA

Silly man. The thought of any of my Blood silently enduring the pain of an unspoken need made my heart ache. Let alone that Tlacel had actually been *afraid* to tell me for fear that I'd think less of him.

The man had shredded tendons and broken bones to keep me and Xochitl from falling through the portal. I didn't doubt his dedication, love, or strength in any way. Even if he wanted me to tie him up so he couldn't move a muscle.

Itztli stepped away a moment and quickly returned with a coil of white rope. Still gripping Tlacel's neck hard with my right hand, I touched the rope with my other to judge its strength. It was surprisingly soft and flexible despite its thickness. The only problem: I didn't know the best way to tie him up.

Tying his wrists together was too basic. Too... normal.

My feathered serpent Blood wanted so much more than that. In his bond, he'd wanted to be wrapped up so tightly that he couldn't move a muscle, almost like a cocoon.

Guillaume stepped out from the fringe of Blood around the room and joined us. "If I may make some suggestions..."

Itztli handed him the coiled rope. "Be our guest."

Letting the ends of the rope fall to the floor, Guillaume shifted his hands to roughly the middle of the length. He tugged on the rope, testing its strength, and nodded. "It's a good choice. With the correct knots and positions, even our alpha would have a hard time breaking free without shifting to his rock troll. Turn him around, my queen."

I'd never really thought about how much stronger I was physically than a normal human. I'd come into my power, sure, but all my Blood were bigger and badder than me. Except not really, because with a hard twist of my hand, I had Tlacel turned away from me.

All of my Blood would try to anticipate my wishes and act before I ever had to ask them, let alone force them. But Tlacel wanted a little bit of that force. He *wanted* me to put him where I wanted him—and then force him to stay there.

I watched as Guillaume looped the rope around each of Tlacel's arms at the elbow, drawing his arms back impossibly far. I kept careful attention on his bond, listening for any real pain or concern. His shoulders strained and pulled, but the ache made a soft sigh escape his lips. His heart thudded heavily and his cock twitched between us. All I had to do was look at one of the guys and he was erect, but Tlacel was definitely getting into this. The tip of his cock glistened and his breathing came faster. I didn't have to see his eyes to know they were heavy and dark with lust.

Guillaume looped the rope up the man's biceps, keeping his muscles taut with strain as his arms were encased.

Unsheathing a knife, he cut off both ends, giving us two shorter sections to work with.

"I'm assuming you want him... *accessible*," G said as he waggled his eyebrows, making me laugh. "Put him where you want him, and then we'll tie up his legs to make him as uncomfortable as possible."

Itztli helped me ease his brother down to his knees, and then he and G each used a piece of rope to bind Tlacel's ankles tightly to his thighs. The rope dug into his skin, making the muscle bulge on either side of the binding. It looked fairly uncomfortable, but I supposed that was the point. I walked around Tlacel, listening to his bond and making sure he wasn't in too much pain.

"How did you learn to do this?" I asked Guillaume.

"A benefit of being imprisoned for so long. The guards had to get inventive with their restraints." Guillaume grabbed a handful of Tlacel's hair and tugged his head back, bending his throat in a hard arc. A gasp escaped his throat and he swallowed hard. "Another time, you might want to tie his hair to his hands, like this. And of course, you could always bind his balls or cock too. Some guys really enjoy that, but again, I assumed you would want him accessible and ready to use without having to untie him first. You'll need to be more careful with such tender bits."

Mehen snorted at *tender bits*, but I felt Rik give him a hard alpha nudge before he could say anything. Even a good-natured joke might hurt Tlacel's confidence, though as I listened to his bond, all I felt was a scorching wildfire racing through his body. He didn't care about what the other Blood might think of him right now.

"Thank you, G."

My knight inclined his head and quietly withdrew, leaving me alone with the twins in the center of the room. Casually, I walked back around in front of Tlacel so I could see his face. His lips were parted, his chest heaving. Sweat glistened on his skin, smearing the paint. His eyes...

I'd thought they'd be heavy and burning with desire, but instead, his eyes were soft and unfocused. Exactly how Daire looked when one of the guys manhandled him. Bottomed out and drifting away into bliss.

Stepping closer, I cupped Tlacel's chin in my hand and waited until he blinked and focused on my face. Without looking away from him, I said, "Itztli, you can help me undress while your brother watches."

Itztli immediately seized the bottom hem of my sweater and tugged it up over my head. I hadn't bothered with a bra. Tlacel's eyes dropped to my breasts and his shoulders quivered, tendons standing out beneath his skin. Torture, to be so close to me and not be able to touch me.

Exactly what he wanted.

Itztli's fingers moved to the button on my jeans. I closed my fingers over his, stilling his movements.

"Slowly," I whispered, tipping my head to the side in invitation. "Give him a good show."

He stepped closer to my back, pressing the heat of his upper body against me. I let out a rumbling purr of pleasure and nestled deeper into his arms, making sure to rub my ass up good and tight against his dick. He dipped his head and kissed the side of my neck, his lips soft and gentle as he roamed up toward my ear. Goose bumps raced down my arms, making me shiver.

He lingered on the hollow behind my ear, licking my skin and lightly sucking on that spot. My knees trembled, and he caught me up fully against him, one big arm wrapped around my waist, his other around my upper body so he could palm my breast. He rubbed and squeezed me gently, using his fingers to scissor around my nipple.

Heat pooled in my abdomen and I rocked against him. I

arched my neck to the other side, inviting his mouth to torment the opposite side of my neck. Though instead of soft kisses, this time he scratched his fangs teasingly down my throat. He worked the muscle that ran across the top of my shoulder, gripping me with his teeth like a jaguar will hold his mate.

"Yes," I whispered, encouraging him to sink his fangs in me. I wanted him inside me. I wanted to feel his hunger surging through our bond. His power rising as my blood filled his mouth.

But first, he tugged on the button of my jeans, and this time, I let him.

He hooked his thumbs in the waistband and with agonizing slowness, he worked the tight denim down my hips. Dropping to his knees behind me, he licked a leisurely path down my back. He kissed the delicate hollows on either side at the base of my spine as he helped me step out of my jeans.

Nuzzling my buttocks, he pressed his tongue deep between my cheeks, pushing me forward. I grabbed Tlacel's shoulders, bracing myself as Itztli dipped lower and tasted my cream. Spreading heat and moisture through my entire body, he dragged his tongue back up my crack. Down again, nudging me harder, until I held onto his brother's shoulders for dear life.

Which put my breasts closer to Tlacel's face. He leaned in as much as he could, desperate to touch me any way he could, even while he was bound. His mouth burned on my skin, hot and desperate, his fangs sharp and throbbing in our bond, but I wasn't ready to let him feed yet. The taste of my blood had made him come before, and we'd only just begun the delicious torment.

I fisted my fingers in his hair and jerked his head back. "No fangs. Not yet."

His chest heaved, his face flushed, but he nodded. "Yes, my queen."

I dropped down to my knees before him and he trembled in the ropes. His cock strained to reach me, its head dark purple and leaking fluid. "How long can you endure my mouth while your brother fucks me?"

Another tremor shook him, his voice ragged as he said, "As long as it takes, my queen."

TLACEL

I'd dreamed of being helpless for our queen. Tied up. Unable to move. I'd fantasized about her making me watch while she fucked another Blood. Even my brother.

But never in a million years had I dared imagine that she'd include me like this. That she'd embrace my need—and still want to touch me. Still want... *me*. At all.

Yet here my powerful, gorgeous queen knelt in front of me, leaning down low so she could lick the tip of my dick.

She could have ordered her alpha to please her. Or one of the other men, all larger than life and bolder than me. Even silent Xin or easy-going Nevarre would have been a better choice than me. At least that's what my brain tried to tell me.

Though it was fucking hard to think with my queen's mouth tormenting me.

She hummed with my dick on her tongue, nearly blowing the top of my skull off, and Itztli hadn't even thrust inside her yet. He was too busy worshipping our queen's ass to care about my torment. Gripping her hips, he lifted her knees up off the floor so he could get his tongue deeper inside her.

The deeper he worked his tongue...

The harder she sucked me.

Her fangs were hard and cold against my flesh,

sliding perilously over my tender skin. The silent threat made me shudder, my muscles aching with strain. A vicious cramp tore through my thigh. Groaning, I tried to twist my wrists to gain even a centimeter of space, but the headless knight knew his way around ropes as well as he knew his many blades. I couldn't even rip my skin open and use blood as a lubricant to loosen the bindings.

All I could do was kneel there and shudder and hope that the sounds I made didn't drive our queen away to one of her more dominant Blood.

She came up for air and seized my face in both hands, her fingers digging into my cheeks. Her eyes gleamed with a furious glint that made my heart stutter in my chest. "The only dominant Blood I need is my alpha, and if I wanted to tie Rik up and torment him like this, he'd let me. In a heartbeat. Because he loves me, and I love him. So why should it be any different for you?"

My chest heaved, my heart too heavy in my chest. I couldn't breathe. But somehow, I forced the words out. "It'd be different if *you* wanted it."

"What makes you think I don't want this? That I don't want you?"

I couldn't answer. I couldn't form the words. Her bond swelled inside my head, spilling over with a wealth of emotions and the brutal, naked truth. She loved the fuzzy look in my eyes. Every time I whimpered or cried out, her clit throbbed. And when she thought of sinking her fangs into me... pleasure shimmered in her.

She was close to coming. My queen. Just from tormenting me.

Licking her lips, she dipped her shoulders down again and inhaled my dick. My breath hissed out, a startled groan shredding my throat. And then I felt the surge in our bond.

Pleasure crested inside her and erupted into a sparkling fountain that cascaded through us both.

Itztli wasn't touching her. He wasn't fucking her. That pleasure was solely from her reaction to me.

I met my brother's gaze, sure that my eyes glistened with tears. But no shame. Not now. Not ever again.

Itztli's eyes glittered like an obsidian mirror, reflecting the truth back at me. This was me. This was my queen.

And she loved me more than ever.

"Which is why she's *our* queen, brother. Forever."

Her bond flowed through me like dancing quicksilver. *:I want you inside me, my obsidian blade. And when I come again, my feathered serpent, we'll fly through the night together on your wings.:*

Gripping her hips, Itztli thrust deep, jostling her mouth on my dick. The slight movement rubbed her fangs on me, sending my nerves screeching with delicious sensation. Yes, it was terrifying, the thought of her brutal fangs tearing me up, but it was also arousing. It was just another way that she made me helpless. That she used me, for her pleasure, not mine.

Itztli smoothed one palm up her back, smearing streaks of white and black on her skin. I wanted to paint her like this. Her dark, shining eyes catching mine every once in a while, as she lifted her mouth. Her long hair loose about her beautiful face, sliding over my skin like silk. The treacherous curves of her spine and hips. My brother's fingers denting her skin, his grip fierce. His jaws tense, shoulders straining as he fought to restrain his own needs.

But he shouldn't have worried. Our queen knew us inside and out. She reached back and plunged her silver-tipped nails into his thigh, giving him the pain he needed, while letting her feed at the same time.

Our twin bonds had always been entangled. His pleasure,

mine. His fears, mine. Even his pain, though it never stirred my lust like his. I felt the growing explosion at the base of his spine, and it matched my approaching release. The kind of climax that rocked the foundations of your world, mixed up with down, and razed everything to the ground.

I felt the jerk of my brother's hips as climax pulsed through him. I tasted him in our queen's bond as she sucked up his blood through her unique nails. And then I felt her release blooming in a sudden explosion of heat. She jerked her mouth off my dick and sank her fangs deeply into my thigh above the rope.

My blood mingled with my brother's. She fed on us at the same time. She made us come at the same time, because I couldn't resist the pleasure that torched through me whenever she fed. She sucked me down, sweeping me up into the night sky, just as she'd promised. Though it wasn't my wings that carried her, but the dark, powerful wings of her flying jaguar.

It took me a long time to find my way back to my body. I slowly became aware of her head pillowed on my thigh, her arms around my waist. Her fingers stroked over the deeply embedded marks the ropes had left in my thighs. I'd fallen over at some point, though she and my brother must have caught me.

I felt a tug as Guillaume sliced through the ropes binding my arms. I couldn't move them, not yet. Everything tingled as blood rushed to my fingers. My muscles creaked and ached with every movement, a deep, delicious throb that made me groan, and yeah, my cock stirred again. I'd never cared for pain before, but this muscle ache was damned good.

For the first time in my very long life, I felt completely at peace. No secret doubt harbored deep inside me. No fear that she might change her mind and turn aside if she saw the truth. She saw me. She saw everything. And she was still here, one hand lazily stroking my back as my brother massaged my arms and checked my fingers to make sure they hadn't kept me tied up too long.

I wasn't surprised when Rik joined us. Her alpha dropped to the floor and shifted her lower body up onto him rather than the floor. However, I was shocked when Mehen dropped down beside me and pushed into the pile of bodies. The grumpy dragon wasn't usually one for cuddling, especially if he hadn't been involved in the sex.

Mehen caught her hand that was still tracing the grooves in my thigh and lifted her fingers to his mouth. "You can tie up my tender bits as long as you kiss and stroke the marks to make them all better later."

She laughed softly and rubbed her thumb along his bottom lip. "That could be arranged, my dragon, though you don't have to do anything you don't like to get my mouth on you."

I could see the image in my head. Mehen's dark skin, his long body stretched out flat. Scales glittering in his arms and shoulders like embedded emeralds. His eyes blazing green fire. While our queen looked up at me, her hair dragging over his groin. A secretive, sensual heat in her eyes as she tied a bow around his dick.

"Done," Mehen said immediately. "Start painting."

4

QUEEN TAKES A LATE CHRISTMAS

(Written after Queen Takes Checkmate, set before Queen Takes Triune)
Be sure to read the freebie Princess Takes Unicorns first!

SHARA

"Um, guys?" Daire shielded his eyes against the sunlight bouncing off the snow. "Do my eyes deceive me, or is there a rhinoceros running across the lawn?"

After a leisurely ride home from Kansas City, we were headed out to visit the crow queen and her flock who'd nested in my grove. Surely he was joking, but Rik jerked me up in his arms and roared. "Intruder!"

The rest of my Blood shifted in a flurry of teeth, claws, and wings. Leviathan exploded up into the air with a belching plume of smoke. Vivian shifted into her flaming phoenix. My gryphon shrieked an ear-splitting warning. Ezra roared, Itztli howled, Daire snarled—

And a child laughed. "Look at me! I'm a unicorn!"

Xochitl? My heart leaped up into my throat. "Stand down, everyone! Xochitl? How did you get here?"

Rik set me down in front of him, and I stepped around my grizzly's massive bulk so I could see. Like Daire, I couldn't believe my eyes. A rhinoceros did indeed run toward us, along with a white pony. Her mane and tail were pink and purple. Sparks flew up from the ground every time she took a step. And yes, a large crystal horn sprouted from her forehead.

Laughing, she stomped a merry circle around me, casting rainbows glittering up into the air. "Through the tree, silly."

Through the tree...

I looked out toward the ancient trees that surrounded my manor house. The central heart tree's limbs spread low to the ground, dotted with wicked thorns and roses, even in dead of winter. I'd died on that tree to power my grove, and my blood flowed through its roots. After admiring the Zaniyah grotto in Mexico, I'd returned home to find a similar hot spring bubbling up from the roots of the heart tree. Its trunk had split open into a dark hole, but the tree seemed fine otherwise.

I'd seen quetzals from Mexico flying in and out of my tree, so it was certainly a possibility that she'd traveled through some kind of portal. She'd almost been taken through a cenote portal in Mexico, and we'd used portals in Egypt to reach Heliopolis so I could face Ra. Evidently, we now had a portal between my nest and Zaniyah's, which I had to admit, could come in handy. If I ever needed my sibling queen...

:Mayte, Xochitl is paying me a visit.:

Her bond jolted with alarm. *:What? How?:*

:She's here. She said she came through the tree. And she brought a... rhinoceros with her.:

:He's her Blood.:

Now it was my turn to ask, *:What? How? She's only a child.:*

:I mentioned we'd had some excitement around here, but I haven't had time to tell you the details. I'm going to try the tree myself and see if I can reach you.:

Xochitl bumped me with her nose to get my attention. "This is my friend, Keras. He's a king rhino."

"Hello, Keras." He snorted and ducked his head, but evidently he couldn't speak like Xochitl. "So you came through the tree?"

"Uh huh," she replied. "Just like when Isis came to take me to rescue him."

Ah, that would explain much. I cupped her head in my hands and searched her gleaming eyes that shimmered with all the colors of the rainbow. "The goddess came to you?"

"We went to get Keras and then She made me a unicorn. Look at my horn! I can stab the bad guys with it! When I'm older, She said I could have wings too."

"I'm so glad that you came to see me, but you should always let your mother know first. That way my mean dragon doesn't try to roast your Blood."

She hung her head and sighed. "I wanted to surprise you. Mama's real mad."

Indeed, Mayte's bond buzzed like a nest of angry hornets. "She loves you very much, and she almost lost you just a few weeks ago."

"I know. But it's so *boring*." She heaved a sigh like boredom was a fate worse than death. "Mama won't let me go anywhere or do anything."

"Well, the good news is that the sun god is dead, so he won't try to steal you again. I'm sure your mother will be more comfortable letting you explore outside the nest now."

:My sister has exited the tree along with Tepeyollotl, my queen,:
Tlacel reported in the bond.

In a few moments, I could see them myself. Xochitl took
one look at their faces and stepped behind me. Mayte's bond
still simmered with a mother's worry, and a thunderstorm
brewed in her jaguar god's dark eyes.

"Xochitl, come here," Mayte said firmly.

Hanging her head, the unicorn did as she was asked,
though each step dragged with reluctance.

"What were you thinking?" Tepeyollotl's voice rolled with
the power of an earthquake.

Xochitl sniffed and tears dripped from her eyes. "I'm
sorry, Papa. I wanted to see Queen Shara and show her my
gift from her goddess."

Mayte looped her arm around her daughter's neck and gave
her a hug. "But you should have told us first. You can't just pop
into our queen's nest without asking. It's rude and dangerous."

"I'm sorry, Your Majesty," Xochitl said in a quavering
voice. "I wanted to surprise you and ask you something."

I dropped down to one knee before her and smoothed the
mane back out of her eyes. "What did you wish to ask,
sweetheart?"

"Did you have Christmas?"

Surprised, I tried to think back that far. It had only been a
few weeks, but a load of shit had gone down since Christmas.
I'd acquired several more Blood, grown the grove, gone to
Mexico, killed the queen of New York City, and then hunted
down Ra, the god of light, and smoked his ass in his own
legendary city of Heliopolis. Somewhere in there, we'd had
two major holidays. "Yes, of course."

"What did Santa Claus bring you?"

We'd had a delightful Christmas orgy in the moonlight
while I laid the blood circle around my nest, but I couldn't

tell the child that. "Santa brought me my dragon and my raven Blood."

She glanced up at the two Blood slowly wheeling over us. Leviathan dwarfed all my other winged Blood, but she didn't seem too impressed. "But did you have any presents? Mama's Blood always make something to give her. That's her rule. They have to make it themselves. No shopping allowed. But they still wrap everything up and sometimes make it a game for her to find all the presents. Did they do something like that for you?"

"Not exactly, but that sounds like a really nice tradition. Maybe we can do that next Christmas."

Her eyes widened and she looked at her mother and then back to me. "You didn't have any presents to unwrap? Not one?"

I kissed her soft muzzle. "I would rather have my Blood any day."

She cocked her head slightly and then nodded. "Yeah. Me too. Keras is fun to play with."

Smiling, I stood back up. "I'm glad you have a friend."

"Home with you, young lady," Mayte said firmly. "And next time, you must let me know before you go inside the tree, so I can contact our queen and make sure she's home and available to see you."

"Yes, Mama. But wouldn't it be easier if I could tell her myself?"

I would need to taste the child's blood to complete the bond and make her a formal sibling. "Let's discuss that when you're older, alright? Then if you still want to do so, you can become my queen sibling like your mother."

Mayte lifted her chin and tipped her head my direction, giving her daughter a stern look.

"Yes, Your Majesty," Xochitl replied dutifully.

I leaned down and whispered in her ear. "How about you just call me Shara?"

Her eyes lit up but she looked at her mother first. "May I, Mama?"

"Not until you're older." Xochitl's head drooped again, and Mayte quirked her lips. "You may call her Aunt Shara until you're a queen in your own right."

Her head jerked up and she hopped around me excitedly, filling the air with sparkles. "Aunt Shara! Aunt Shara!"

Tepeyollotl gave her a playful swat on her rump. "Off to home with you, butterfly. The queens have business to discuss."

"Yes, Papa." She reared up and gently braced her hooves on my shoulders so she could give me a pony kiss. Then she tore off toward the trees, her tail flowing in the wind. "Race you, Keras!"

The rhinoceros gave me a long-suffering look and blew out a disgusted snort, but he trotted after her.

Mayte kissed her jaguar god on the cheek. "Thank you, my heart. I'll be along soon."

He inclined his head to me politely. "Your Majesty."

I blinked and he was suddenly a gigantic black jaguar. His eyes flashed in the sunlight like obsidian mirrors. He streaked across the snow after his daughter, distracting her so the heavier rhino could catch up.

Smiling, I met Mayte's gaze. "I'm glad she discovered the tree would connect our nests. Now you can come whenever you wish."

"Me too," she admitted sheepishly. "But she needs to follow a few rules too, or I'm not going to survive until she's a queen of her own nest."

"So what's up?"

"Oh, nothing, really. He just said we had business to discuss to distract her."

"And maybe he wanted to give you some time away?"

She smiled fondly. "Yes, probably. We've all been on edge. Xochitl has felt so constrained and trapped lately. It's a relief for all of us that you were successful."

"Do you want to go up to the house? I'm sure Winston has a pot of tea or coffee on."

"Where were you going before Xochitl interrupted?"

"I was going down to the heart tree."

"You could show her your grotto," Rik suggested. "It was inspired by hers."

Mayte's eyes lit up. "I was too busy chasing after Xochitl to notice. You have a grotto too?"

"Yes, it's magical. Literally. I came home from your nest and it was here. Is Keras really her Blood?"

Mayte looped her arm with mine as we walked back the way she'd come to the grove. "Yes, they've completed the initial blood exchange. Obviously, nothing more until they're older, but she's able to help him control when he shifts. He's only eight years old and on his own, until Xochitl found him."

My heart ached so badly that I didn't try to speak for a few moments. My dragon had been exiled even younger. A child, alone in the world, without even an orphanage or foster home to take him in. For kings who could shift at will, there were few places of safety, especially when their own families were afraid to keep them. "I'm glad you were able to help him."

"Me too. He's been such a joy to have around, and not just because he helps entertain Xochitl. Though they're definitely becoming fast friends."

The path became more rocky as we neared the heart tree, and the snow melted away beneath the warmer ground. Steam curled in the air above the hot spring bubbling up from the roots of the tree. Rose-laden limbs hung around the sides and red petals floated on the water, providing gentle perfume even in winter.

"Oh, Shara," she breathed out. "This is gorgeous."

"Do you have time for a soak?"

She flashed a sultry smile at me as her fingers moved to the zipper of her dress. "With you? Always."

"Wait." I stepped closer and captured her hands. "Xochitl said I should have presents to unwrap."

Mayte laughed softly and turned around, peeking at me over her shoulder. "So I'm your extremely late Christmas present? That's the nicest compliment anyone has ever given me. But who's going to unwrap you, my queen?"

My lips quirked. "Would you like to meet my newest Blood?"

As soon as I mentioned her, my phoenix dropped down beside us in a fiery streak, shifting back to her human form as she landed on the rocky edge. Her long red hair cascaded around her like a burning curtain of silk, her black skin glistening with her internal flames.

"Mayte Zaniyah, this is my Blood, Vivian Heliopolis."

Vivian inclined her head, but there was nothing soft about her. Her lean, hard body was all sharp angles and steely muscles.

"Wow." Mayte's eyes widened. "We met briefly in your dream, my queen."

I listened to her bond, and almost changed my mind. Her heart... quavered. Like she was afraid. I never wanted anyone to be afraid of joining me, even in a sexual feeding frenzy. I'd only thought Vivian could provide some extra guidance since Mayte and I were both relatively new to pleasuring women, but if it made her uncomfortable... "Would you mind if she joins us?"

She started, her gaze flickering to mine guiltily. "Not at all. She's just very... formidable."

Vivian let out a dark, silky chuckle that made goosebumps race down my arms. "That's the nicest compliment anyone has ever given me, too. Perhaps I should focus all my attention on you, my queen, and leave your sweet sibling alone."

I finished unzipping Mayte's dress and she turned around to face us, her arms holding up the bodice of her gown. She looked up at me shyly through her long, brown hair, her eyes soft and luminous. "There's a side to me that you haven't seen yet, Shara. It's... embarrassing. I don't want you to think less of me."

I cupped her cheeks in both hands and pressed my forehead to hers. "What on earth would give you that idea? I love what we have, Mayte. I love you. You're like a sister that I always wished for, but even better, because we can give each other pleasure too. But if you're scared..."

"I'm not scared." Despite her words, her voice quivered, making my eyes narrow with concern. "Not exactly." She blew out a sigh, her gaze locking on my lips. "Do you remember the presentation dinner? And the way that Daire looked at you?"

That night, Daire had been his normal flirtatious self, though he'd gone one step further and invited punishment. He'd wanted to be taken well in hand. In fact, Mehen had done exactly that after we retired to my room. He'd manhandled Daire with an impressive wrestling match, ending with him forcing Daire into submission.

Which was exactly what my warcat had wanted.

Understanding dawned on me. Mayte had a softness about her that I loved. Vivian had a natural hardness.

"I've not always been in touch with my more submissive side," Mayte said softly. "I was ashamed of it. I was afraid that if I revealed my true nature that my Blood would think me weak and unable to protect the nest. You're my queen, Shara.

I'll gladly give you anything you want and love every minute of it. Especially if Vivian wouldn't mind exerting some of that dominance to *make* me pleasure you."

VIVIAN

I tried not to say or do anything that would sway my queen's decision, even though a simmering volcano rumbled inside me.

Shara had already answered my fervent prayer and taken me as her Blood. That she'd even consider allowing me to fuck her sibling queen… Let alone dominate her…

That was a boon that I did not deserve.

Shara gave me a hard look that still managed to be sultry. "You deserve everything you could ever desire and more, my Blood."

I swallowed hard. "I know how you feel about other women touching us, my queen. If you don't want me to touch her…"

Her head tipped slightly and her luscious lips curved. "I'd like you to touch her. Very much. As long as she wants it too."

Mayte let out a fragile breathy sigh that stirred the flames hotter inside me. "I do."

I loved my queen with every furious beat of my heart. I'd slit my throat to please her and bathe the world in hellfire to protect her. But she would never make such a prey-like sound.

A sound my predator liked very much indeed.

While she'd definitely allowed me to guide our love-making to a point, she'd never want to be truly dominated. It just wasn't in her. Even her alpha would never try to exert himself to conquering her will. He could guide, suggest, and on occasion, take the reins at her suggestion, but he'd always do so with finesse and a careful ear to her bond.

Shara fucking Isador loved us and loved fucking us in any way we desired. But none of us would ever expect her to *submit*.

Never.

Whatever Shara gave me was enough. I didn't even consider wanting to dominate her. I was happy enough to have her touch me on occasion and allow me to fuck her without one of her males. It'd never occurred to me in a million years that I'd have the opportunity to dominate another woman ever again. Let alone for our queen's enjoyment.

She loved watching Mehen or Ezra push Daire around.

The thought of her watching *me* dominate Mayte...

And fucking *enjoying* it...

Smoak screeched inside of me, a storm of flames that threatened to ignite the heart tree.

Shara tugged the sweater over her head and tossed it down on the rock ledge that formed a perfect lounging area beside the hot spring. Shoving her jeans down her thighs, she winked at me. "Oh, I'm going to enjoy the hell out of it."

"Stop," I barked out automatically. She arched a brow at my harsh tone, but paused. "My queen," I quickly amended. "May I suggest that you allow Mayte to unwrap you? She's your late Christmas present after all."

Laughing softly, Shara dropped down to sit on top of her sweater with her jeans partially pulled down. "If she's the gift, shouldn't she be the one unwrapped?"

I gazed steadily at Mayte and didn't answer. Entranced, she stared at our queen's breasts and the tip of her tongue moistened her lips. She was a lovely woman with dusky brown skin and luminous eyes, shorter than our queen with lush, soft curves. Even feet away, I could smell her scent of warm, spicy flowers as her temperature rose. Tempting, yes, but I wanted to see how she reacted to me, not just to our queen.

Finally, she lifted those gleaming eyes up to my face and she froze. Her nostrils flared with alarm, her eyes wide as she took in my stance. Even though I kept my hands loose at my sides and made no threatening moves, I couldn't help but radiate command and intimidation, a proud, furious energy that bowed for no one and nothing except our queen.

I didn't say a word. I didn't have to. Mayte dropped to her knees at our queen's feet, but it was *my* silent will that put her there. I stepped closer and seized her nape in my left hand, deliberately tangling her hair in my fingers. She gasped softly, her eyes widening even more. Her pupils dilated, her lips parted, and her smoldering scent of flowers filled my nose.

"Mayte? Are you alright?" Shara asked softly.

I tightened my fingers on Mayte's throat. "Tell her."

"Yes, my queen." Her voice trembled, her chest heaving frantically for air. "This is…"

I gave her a firm, hard shake, squeezing her neck mercilessly. Staring up at me, it was like she melted. Her bones softened. Her muscles pliant. Her eyes shining bottomless pits of need.

Need for me.

I clenched my teeth so hard I was afraid I'd break off a fang.

Mayte sighed. "Perfect."

SHARA

My first instinct was to surge up and pull Mayte to safety. I didn't like hearing that fragile sound on her lips. It was a sound of pain, like a tender animal caught in a wolf's jaws.

But she didn't need my protection, not from this, and certainly not from Vivian.

I leaned back on my elbows, as relaxed as I could be on a hard rock, and told my protective instincts to take a back seat. I'd seen that unmistakable look in Mayte's eyes before— when Daire was getting exactly what he wanted and needed. I trusted Vivian to take care of Mayte. If anything went amiss, I'd know in their bonds.

:Nothing will go amiss.: Vivian's bond reverberated with determination in my head. *:I'll take excellent care of her, and you, my queen.:*

:I know you will.:

She twisted her wrist, wrapping another length of Mayte's hair around her hand. My eyes watered in sympathy. Such a simple but effective way to deliver pain and control. It didn't take violence or weapons.

She gave a firm tug, forcing Mayte to look up at her. "You're going to eat our queen's pussy while I fuck you."

Mayte trembled, her bond smoking hotter with the sweet scent of smoldering jungle flowers. "Yes, please."

Vivian walked her closer on her knees, keeping a tight grip on her head. With trembling fingers, Mayte pulled my jeans and panties the rest of the way down my legs, but she couldn't take them off until she untied my shoes. Naturally one of the laces knotted, forcing her to slow down and concentrate. Sweat beaded on her forehead and she captured her bottom lip in her teeth as she worked. Her fangs hadn't descended yet.

But mine did.

The heavy ache of hunger slowly grew inside me. I hadn't tasted my sibling queen in weeks. I hadn't breathed in her sweet perfume from the silky delicate curve of her throat. I wanted her softness against me. Her sweet, tender spirit entwining with mine.

Vivian huffed out a laugh. "You're not helping her much, my queen."

Startled, I dragged my gaze up from the inviting curve of Mayte's throat to her luminous eyes. Her pupils were dilated so large that her eyes were almost completely black. Her breath panted from her parted lips and sweat glistened on her skin, making her glow even more. Steam curled around us, making me sweat too, but not all of the heat spreading through my body was due to the hot spring.

She muttered a curse and jerked harder at the laces, but finally gave up and just pulled my tennis shoe off. Wrapping her palms around my calves, she snagged my jeans and finally pulled them off.

I sat up enough to grab our discarded clothes to use as a pillow. Lying back, I opened my thighs, adjusting the makeshift cushion so I could still watch.

Vivian gave another firm tug on Mayte's hair, keeping her upright rather than burying her face between my thighs immediately. "Stay."

Releasing her, Vivian started to undress. Unhurried, she untied each heavy boot, stripped off her black leather pants, and tugged the tank top over her head. Her movements were controlled and precise, even though her bond crackled like a bonfire. Flames licked inside her, eager to burst free into a blazing conflagration. The air around her shimmered, her phoenix shining like a fiery aura around her.

She squatted beside me and leaned down slightly in invitation. I rose up on my elbows so I could kiss her. Her scent of burning myrrh and cinnamon rolled over me, so strong and pungent that it almost made me dizzy. My fangs throbbed so hard that I couldn't hold back a soft groan.

Her lips curved against mine in a smug smile and then she raised her head. "Did you hear that, Mayte? Our queen hungers. You may entertain her now."

Their hair trailed over my skin. Mayte's soft tendrils tickled my thighs. The silk of Vivian's hair slid over my breasts. The fullness of her lips against mine as she dipped her head for another kiss. Her lips and hair were the only soft elements on her glorious lean, hard body. I stroked my hands over her shoulders and arms, enjoying the coiled tension in her muscles. So fierce. So strong. Yet her lips were incredibly tender against mine.

She didn't shove her tongue into my mouth or take control of the kiss, even though she could have. It was one small way that she demonstrated her willingness to serve me. Only me.

Mayte's tongue traced a warm, wet trail over my pubic bones and the crease of my thigh. She flattened her tongue against me and licked the entire length of my pussy. My thigh muscles quivered, and I arched up against her mouth. Both of their mouths, because Vivian deepened her kiss too. Her tongue thrust inside my mouth leisurely, flicking my fangs teasingly. I tightened my grip on her neck and tipped my head back, opening to her as surely as my thighs were open for Mayte.

One sucked on my clit, while the other sucked on my tongue and stroked the roof of my mouth, applying subtle pressure that made my fangs descend even more. Blood filled my mouth, both Vivian's and mine. She shuddered, her fingers tightening on my nape where she supported my head. Mayte groaned against my clit, ramping the sensations up another notch. My climax rolled through our bonds and she slipped her tongue inside me, drinking from my core.

As my breathing steadied, Vivian gently lowered me back to the pile of clothes. Licking her lips, she straightened to her full height. Her head tipped back, and Smoak shimmered around her. She didn't transform completely into the phoenix, but I could see the hint of flames hovering over her. She stepped behind Mayte and the flames brightened into liquid red-gold that flowed over her skin like a wetsuit.

"I've been experimenting with something." She stroked her fingers over the gleaming fire rippling across her lower stomach and the flames coalesced into a rod that gleamed like molten steel fresh from the forge. "It doesn't burn me, but I don't know if it'll hurt you."

Mayte nuzzled me with her nose, refusing to lift her head, but she did raise her hand up over her shoulder. Vivian took her hand and carefully touched one of her fingers to the fiery rod. When Mayte didn't pull back in pain, Vivian wrapped the woman's hand around it and pulled it through her fingers like a dick.

"Wow." Mayte whispered as she pressed soft kisses over my flesh. "It's hot, but it doesn't burn. What's it made of?"

"Phoenix flesh. Smoak is letting me borrow his cock in exchange for the pleasure we'll all feel."

Mayte looked up at me, a sly smile tugging on the corner of her mouth. "When I chased after my daughter, I never thought I'd be fucked by a phoenix."

I threaded my fingers in her hair and rubbed my thumb against her lush lips. "Neither did I."

I watched as Vivian dropped to her knees and moved closer to Mayte with the gleaming dick in her hand. I scooted lower, wrapping my thighs around hers so my calves touched Vivian's legs too as she slowly thrust inside.

Vivian's eyes flared wide and a guttural cry escaped her lips. "Holy fuck, that's incredible."

"Mmmm." Mayte hummed deep in her chest. She rocked her hips back, taking Vivian deeper.

I cupped her cheeks, enraptured by the beautiful scene. Mayte taking her pleasure. Vivian's awestruck enjoyment. And yes, Smoak's fiery glee. I could see flaming wings rising up over Vivian's shoulders, though the phoenix didn't take complete control.

"Please," Mayte whispered raggedly. "Feed on me when we come."

Vivian's hips moved more confidently, driving harder, making Mayte's breath whoosh out with every heavy thrust. I pressed my lips to her throat but I didn't bite her. Not yet. I scratched my fangs across the delicate skin and pressed my tongue to her thundering pulse. In her bond, I felt the searing pressure of Vivian's thrusts. Flames licked inside Mayte, intensifying her pleasure without burning her. Vivian pressed one palm between Mayte's shoulder blades and leaned hard against her, pinning her against me. Her other hand squeezed Mayte's hip mercilessly.

Her breath caught. Vivian grabbed a handful of Mayte's hair, jerking her head back so her throat was bared in a hard curve for me.

I sank my fangs deeply into her pulsing vein. Jerking between us, Mayte cried out with pleasure. Sweet, hot blood filled my mouth, flavored with her flowers and jungle fruits, but with a hot, roasted component that was new. She tasted slightly different, like grilled, warm peaches baked into a delicious pie.

Smoak screeched with release and flames poured through our bonds. I could taste smoldering cinnamon and myrrh in Mayte's blood, as if I was feeding on Vivian's blood too.

Mayte nestled her face against my shoulder with a sated sigh of pleasure, her weight settling against me. Her skin was damp with sweat, her cheeks flushed as if she had a fever, but she wasn't burned or injured by Smoak's flames. Panting, Vivian pressed her cheek against Mayte's shoulders and sagged against us. I was delightfully squished beneath them both.

"Sorry," Vivian gasped. "My queen."

"My only complaint is that I didn't get to feel Smoak first."

Vivian's head jerked up, her eyes tight with worry. "Forgive me—"

I reached up and pressed my fingers to her lips. "I'm teasing. I'm beyond pleased that we three were able to share such a wonderful moment together."

Mayte shifted against me and winced as she untangled herself enough to drop down beside me. "Though maybe next time we could do this in a bed. This rock is rather unforgiving on my knees."

Vivian grunted in agreement. "Me too. Though I'd roll around in crushed glass and razorblades for the chance to do this again."

Mayte laughed softly. "Me too."

My two women cuddled against me. One soft and cuddly and sweet. One fierce and hard and just as sweet. Though Vivian's tender moments might not be as frequent, they were more meaningful because I knew what it cost her to let me peek inside her heart. I kissed both of them on the head and tightened my arms around them. "It might be a few weeks late, but this was a wonderful Christmas present."

Mayte pulled away with a regretful sigh and reached over for her discarded dress. "As delightful as this has been, I must get back before Xochitl gallops off into more mischief."

I sat up and Vivian wrapped her arms around my waist, curling around me. "Should we place guards on either tree to keep people from wandering inside accidentally?"

"I don't think that will be necessary," Mayte replied as she tugged her dress over her head. "I was only able to bring Tepeyollotl with me when I held his hand. Xochitl and I both carry your blood. I think that's what opened the portal to you."

I nodded, combing my fingers through Vivian's silky hair. "That makes sense."

Rik's bond rumbled softly in my head like distant thunder. *:We will still guard the tree to be safe, my queen.:*

I smiled. Of course, my alpha would always go above and beyond to secure my safety.

Mayte stepped closer, her eyes shining with soft love that made my heart clench. Leaning down, she brushed her lips over mine. "Thank you, my queen. That was incredible."

"No, thank *you*. I agree wholeheartedly. Do you need to feed before you go back?"

She hesitated, her eyes going distant for a moment. Then she sighed and straightened. "I'd love to, but I'm afraid we'd get distracted again, and Xochitl has convinced my Blood to have a tea party. If I don't rescue them soon, she'll have them all wearing tutus and tiaras while she paints their fingernails in glitter."

Picturing big, strong men like Tepeyollotl and Eztli, Mayte's alpha, dressed up for a tea party made me snicker. "Oh, boy. That sounds fun. I can only imagine…"

My words fell off as the image filled my head. My Blood, all formidable monsters in their own right. Wearing pink fluffy tutus and sparkly crowns, sitting around a child's play table with miniature teacups held precariously in their powerful hands. Held captive by a little girl with dark hair and eyes.

Like mine.

:In a heartbeat,: Rik whispered fervently in my head.

Affirmatives from each of my Blood echoed in our bonds. Even Ezra. *:Though I refuse to act out Goldilocks.:*

:You will if she asks, furball,: Mehen retorted. *:We all will. Even though you're the only bear.:*

Ezra grunted. *:If I'm going to wear a fucking tutu, it'd better be blue or purple at least. I fucking hate pink.:*

I'd never considered having a child, but that image—combined with the aching tenderness in my Bloods' bonds—made me melt. I was still young to be a mother, even for a human, and barely more than a baby myself by Aima standards. But if I never had a daughter, Isis's line would die out with me.

Even more, I'd never give my Blood the opportunity to love a child. Because they would. Wholeheartedly. They would love my daughter as much as they loved me.

I watched as Mayte stepped into the tree. She paused and glanced back to blow a kiss at me, and then she was gone. Back to her home and her daughter.

Closing my eyes, I connected to my heart tree. I felt the rough bark inside me. The piercing of the thorns. My blood flowed deeply into the ground through the network of roots that interlaced with the rest of the grove.

Xochitl's laughter still echoed through the trees, a child's light-hearted joy.

:Someday,: I promised.

House Isador would have a child laughing and dancing beneath these trees.

5

QUEEN TAKES TENTACLES

Special thanks to Jessica Caldwell for adding "Bottom of the Deep Blue Sea" and Heather Estabrook for "Angel" to my playlist for this story.
(Set after Queen Takes Triune)

SHARA

My stomach growled. Before I could open my eyes, I heard the door open.

"Breakfast and news for our queen," Vivian said.

Her bond sparked with flames, but she didn't seem angry or worried. Sitting up, I swiped my hair out of my eyes. Rik stacked a couple of pillows behind me so I could lean back and eat comfortably. Xin pulled up the comforter to cover my legs, and Vivian set the tray onto my lap. I looked around the room quickly to see who else was present.

Mehen and Guillaume stood near the large windows. Ezra and Daire stood at the door. Outside, I could feel Llewellyn and Nevarre circling the nest, sharp eyes watching for anything unusual. The twins were further away but inside my blood circle.

Okeanos was soaking in the grotto, giving his skin a much-needed drink. Though he didn't like the water so hot, he didn't make a single complaint.

Sitting on the edge of the bed, Vivian lifted the silver lid, letting delicious steam waft up. "Crepes stuffed with mascarpone and strawberries with a light limoncello sauce," she said, mimicking Winston's prim and proper British butler accent.

"Yum." I picked up my fork, my mouth already watering. "What news?"

Rather than answering, she picked up a tablet and hit play.

News footage started playing with an anchorwoman standing outside on the street. I couldn't tell the location immediately. "Dr. Walsh, have you ever seen anything like this?"

A woman in an elegant pink blouse and white linen jacket spoke. "Not at all, and for several reasons. Primarily, this infestation is shocking because North America and Antarctica are the only continents without a major species of Acrididae. Until today, we haven't had a live sighting of *Caloptenus spretus* since 1902."

"This Rocky Mountain species was supposedly extinct?"

"Yes. So where did this swarm come from? Even more interesting, a swarm is usually a widespread event, covering dozens or even hundreds of square miles. For this swarm to settle *only* on this property is... quite honestly, astounding, especially when we consider their normal habitat was the dryer Great Plains. They've devoured every blade of grass and leaf on this entire block, but they haven't left yet."

The cameraman panned the shot to the property, and I gasped. Bugs crawled everywhere. On the ground. The walls. The fence. The tree trunks. The ground was quite literally moving and crawling.

With locusts.

Vivian smirked. "Does that building look familiar to you, my queen?"

I huffed out a laugh. "Let me guess. This is a seemingly unimportant old mansion in the heart of the French Quarter in New Orleans, right?"

"Bingo. Wait, it gets better."

I focused on the video.

"Are they dangerous to people," the anchorwoman asked.

Dr. Walsh practically clapped her hands with excitement. "They're annoying and can bite, but they're not known to attack people. We've seen birds and small rodents killed by locust swarms before, and these are even larger and in greater number. I'd love to get onto this property and speak to its owner."

As if on cue, a side door flew open and a small group of people raced down the sidewalk. Three men in suits pressed close to a barely visible woman in the middle. They held black umbrellas over her, trying to shield her from the locusts, the cameras, or both.

Not that they helped much at all, because the swarm immediately descended on her with a vicious, loud drone that sounded like microphone feedback. Flailing arms and swinging umbrellas like bats, they hurried to a waiting car parked on the wrong side of the street.

Outside the Dauphine's nest, of course. Because these locusts had been commanded to cover every surface and attack anything that moved *inside* the nest. They weren't merely a nuisance either. All the men had bleeding bites and scratches. Another person broke from the house and raced after them, only to fall, screaming, as the locusts covered them. I couldn't even tell if it was a man or a woman, one of her Blood or merely a human servant.

The Dauphine certainly didn't pause or try to help them. Her men hustled her into the car as the news people raced over.

"Ma'am, are you the owner? Leonie Delafosse? Please, can you tell us what's happening here? Can we investigate your property and find the cause of this swarm?"

Wearing dark sunglasses with a black scarf tied over her hair, Leonie—aka the Dauphine's alter ego—glared into the camera. "Be my guest. I'm never returning to this cursed place."

Vivian set the tablet aside. "There's not much more, other than more people getting chased off by locusts. Where do you think she'll head now?"

I took a bite of the crepe and closed my eyes in bliss. "It doesn't matter. We'll find her again. I told Marne exactly how the Dauphine wards herself. Gina said the Triune offices usually send out a new book once a year or so, though with my ascendency to Triskeles, she thought a new batch would go out within the month. As soon as we get the new book, we'll know exactly where the Dauphine has tried to hide herself again."

"There's more," Rik said. The deep rumble of his voice made me open my eyes so I could see his face. His bond was solid rock. Not upset or worried—but reserved. "There are visitors lining up outside the gate."

My eyes flared. "Visitors? Like who?"

"Potential Blood."

Other than the place of darkness, I hadn't dreamed anything unusual last night. I didn't remember anyone walking my dreams. I certainly hadn't called anyone deliberately. Shrugging, I turned my attention back to my breakfast. "They're not mine. I didn't call anyone."

Rik didn't reply or react, but his intensity remained heavy and focused. All alpha, ready to beat some skulls together if anyone annoyed me.

"We could use more help," Vivian said slowly. "A queen of your stature…"

I sat back with my coffee cup and arched a brow at her. "Nothing has changed. I don't take Blood that I don't love. I can tell you now that none of them are mine."

Rik wrapped his arm around my shoulders, tucking me against him. "Are you sure?"

I knew he only wanted the best for me. Even if I didn't want a bunch of new Blood interfering with our lives. To be sure that none of these visitors were meant to join us, I closed my eyes and focused on the tapestry in my mind. My beautiful manor house rose up in the center, surrounded by impossibly ancient trees. My beloved Blood gleamed like burning rubies and drops of molten blood in my mind. I could feel them all around me, their bonds shining in the darkness of my mind.

My blood circle gleamed like a fiery rope around my nest. A bright knot of lights waited at one end. Brighter than how humans normally showed up on the tapestry, but none of them called to me. None of them glowed any brighter than the others,or drew my attention.

Moving on, I swept over my heart tree that cast sparks up into the night sky of the tapestry. Drops of diamonds and moonlight mixed with crystal rose petals, shining like stars. The still surface of the water at its base reflected the tree and the sparks, endlessly deep as if an ocean stretched beneath it. Cold and deep and blue.

Okeanos dove through that darkness, tentacles sweeping his kraken body effortlessly through the water.

For a moment, my heart stopped.

He's leaving me.

:Never, my queen,: he replied instantly. Contrite, he paused mid-dive, turning back toward the surface of the water. *:I will gladly stay as long as you allow it. I'll submit to the cage when it's time. Or if you'd rather kill me, I'll go to my knees for your knight's blade without hesitation.:*

His whole life had been nothing but misery. Chained in a cage at the bottom of Marne Ceresa's pond for a hundred years. Even his mother, a Skolos Triune queen, hadn't trusted him.

I couldn't blame him for wanting to explore. To taste freedom for the first time in his life. *:Nobody's putting you in a cage or killing you. You're free. If that means you want to leave...:*

:I don't,: he said immediately.

Though I felt the siren call in his bond. The sea beckoned at the bottom of my grotto. I didn't know how it was possible, but I could taste the salt of the ocean. The heated steam of my grotto had cooled.

Maybe that was his power as a king kraken—to open the portal to the sea.

:It's your *power,:* Rik whispered in my mind. *:Our Triskeles queen has gained the power to access any body of water she wishes from her grotto. Is it any surprise after calling such a Blood as him?:*

A kraken. A mythical creature of the sea. Of course, he would want, no *need*, access to the ocean. I didn't want him withering away, pining for dark salty waters of the deep, resigned to my little steamy grotto in Arkansas.

:Go, my kraken.: I stroked my power through his bond gently, like Daire's tail swishing through me. *:Taste the salt of*

the sea. Explore the depths that call you. Return to me when you wish.:

:Then I wish to stay, my queen, by your side for all time.:

Tears burned my eyes. I felt again his hesitant caress on my wrist. Unsure of his place. Afraid to overstep and be sent to the bottom of the lake in chains once more. *:I am with you always. I am with you now. Show me what it's like to dive into the darkness of the deepest oceans. Take me with you.:*

He hesitated, tentacles slowly unfurling in the water like a purple and black flower. I sank deeper into his bond, letting him feel me moving inside him. I tasted the water on his skin, cool and salty and mysterious. He hadn't swum in ocean water in so long that almost didn't remember what it felt like.

Sinking silently deeper, he curled his tentacles tightly to his body. He glided effortlessly through the endless water, gaining speed as the temperature cooled to icy blackness. His bond burned with the fierce joy of a creature doing exactly what he'd been made to do and doing it extremely well. The mighty kraken was a terror of the sea, large enough to bring down any ship, breaking its masts like fragile sticks. For all his immense size and strength, he was also extremely fast. He plummeted past giant sharks like they were statues.

I pulled my mind back slightly, giving him a kiss in the bond. *:Swim free, my kraken. I'll wait for you at the grotto when you're ready.:*

He was too deeply into his beast to send words back to me, but he sent me an image of a full moon, and the waves rising to its call.

I was his moon, pulling his tide back to the shore.

OKEANOS

F reedom was as foreign to me as dry air on my skin and land beneath my feet. I couldn't remember exactly how old I'd been when I first shifted to the uncontrollable beast inside me. Five or six, I thought. Old enough to finally be taken to the sacred beach outside of Mother's nest.

It'd been a stormy night of fierce winds and growling waves that crashed onto the rocks. Wind tore at my hair and whipped my clothes. The smell of salt and ozone in the air made chills race down my spine. Lightning tore the sky and waves sprayed up onto my face. I'd thrown my head back and lifted my arms, waiting for the storm to sweep me away.

Instead, the kraken had boiled up out of me.

I didn't know how many days I'd been gone to the sea. I dreaded the resignation on Mother's face. But it was fear tightening her lips as I stood before her, bare toes dug down into the sand, kelp tangled in my hair, and streaks of dried salt on my skin.

Goddess below. It'd been so wondrous. I couldn't regret my adventure.

Until Mother banished me back to the sea that had called me. She'd cried and hugged me and told me she loved me...

But then she sent me away.

I was still a child, not a kraken. I didn't know how to call the monster back out. I'd almost starved to death before some of her sibs took pity on me and started bringing me food. I lived on the beach for months, maybe years. I had no way of counting the passing of time other than the number of storms that drove me to burrow beneath one of the palm trees that had been torn up partially from the ground, leaving a snug cave behind.

I learned to catch my own crab and small fish. I cracked

open clams and mussels. I climbed for coconuts and bananas. I survived.

Alone. Always alone.

It was hunger for companionship that drove me back to Undina's nest. I ached for home. Someone to talk to. A blanket in the corner of a storage shed. It didn't have to be much.

But I couldn't cross the blood circle.

Her own child, carrying her blood, but forbidden to cross into her nest. Bound from the safety of home.

That awful finality had filled me with rage, freeing the kraken inside me once more, and yes, I demolished everything I could lay tentacles on. I tore up the beaches. I destroyed the fishing grounds and broke the ships into kindling. I leveled every tree on the island that wasn't inside the circle.

The sea rose to my call. Giant waves pounded the shoreline, flooding inside the nest where I couldn't cross. A child's temper tantrum… in the body of a giant sea monster.

When I finally shifted back to my human form, I'd been consumed with guilt and horror. People had died because of me. Our nest had suffered irreparable damage. Even as a boy, I'd recognized that it would take years for the fishing grounds to recover and the fleet to be rebuilt.

So I'd agreed to be caged to protect them. They locked me in a cave on a reef that flooded with salt water at high tide. I learned how to stay in the kraken form—simply to stay alive. The bars were blessed with Undina's magic and etched with runes to keep me contained. They worked, even when I transformed to the kraken.

My family was safe. That was all that mattered.

When Undina came to see me years later, I snapped back to my human form so quickly that I was left shaking and weeping on the rocks. I'd thought she was freeing me. Maybe she'd missed me, or had second thoughts about imprisoning me. Maybe she could love me. Just a little.

Instead, she'd given me to Marne Ceresa, and the last bit of hope I'd ever known had withered up and died. Until my queen freed me from the bottom of that cramped cage and willingly gave me her blood.

I still didn't know why she'd called me as Blood. I would have helped her against the queen of Rome even if she'd left me at the bottom of the pool. I certainly didn't know why she'd *kept* me.

Nor why she'd freed me now.

But I couldn't resist the call of the sea. Cold bottomless depths. Pressure building as I sank like a stone into its salty embrace. I could stretch out my tentacles as far as I wanted, flattening my giant body out to slow my descent. No iron bars. No magical bindings to chain me. Only the whisper of my queen's bond in my head, her sweet promise that she'd be waiting.

Waiting for me.

Even here in these ocean depths, I could feel her. A shining beacon filtering down through miles of dark water. A sweeter call than any legendary siren.

My queen. She'd saved me. She'd freed me. And now... she called me.

Home. To her.

I shot upward effortlessly, parting endless blue until my head broke the surface of the water. Her grotto steamed around me, making my kraken hiss and draw up tightly into a squirming ball of tentacles.

Fuck. I'd forgotten to shift as I neared the surface.

And now that I was here...

I couldn't find my control. I couldn't concentrate. My mind crackled and sparked like a massive lightning storm on the horizon. I was grotesque. She hadn't given me permission to shift. A powerful, formidable queen might use such a creature to defend her nest, but she couldn't possibly want to *keep* me as Blood. Not her. I'd seen how she loved them. I'd seen her feed them and touch them and hold them...

And damn me to the Mariana Trench because I wanted her love too. Even knowing how impossible that foolish longing was.

Shara Isador sat on the rocky ledge, dangling her legs in the steamy water. Smiling. Even when one of my tentacles flopped out completely against my control and brushed her ankle.

She didn't flinch away. She didn't close her eyes and shudder. She didn't turn away or call one of her Blood...

Looking around quickly, it finally dawned on me.

Even the big alpha wasn't present. He'd actually left his precious queen alone. With a monster.

With me.

"Amazing." She reached down and swirled her fingers in the water. My tentacles writhed in bliss as the tiny ripples of her touch cascaded through the water to me. "I can feel how much cooler the water is, and it tastes salty. Hopefully it doesn't kill the tree or the vegetation."

She looked at me, head tilted, as if she expected me to answer. Even though she hadn't asked a question.

Deep and serious, her eyes tugged on my soul, cracking me into a thousand pieces.

"I'm not afraid of you, Okeanos."

:You should be.:

I expected her to laugh nervously or protest a little too firmly that she didn't fear me.

Instead, she slipped into the water.

I slammed back against the rocky side, tentacles scrambling up the ledge to haul myself up and out of the water. I didn't know why. It just felt like she would be safer if I was out of my natural element. On land, the kraken would be severely slowed down and eventually incapacitated without his watery environment.

Even with millions of powerful suction cups, I couldn't grip the slick rocks. Ridiculous, actually. I'd never had issues before with any kind of mossy or watery surface. I was made to grab giant boulders and crack them open. I could tear apart a massive freighter, but today, I couldn't even grip the tree's roots that arched up out of the water and along the rocky ledge.

She swam closer and I pressed tighter against the rocks. Trying to spare her. If I traumatized her...

Laughing softly, she wrapped her fingers around one of the smaller tentacles that lined my giant beak. Involuntarily, it wrapped around her finger and held on for dear life.

"I've seen you as a kraken before. Why are you so concerned now? You're amazing."

:You were in danger before. Now... I'm merely repulsive.:

"Not at all. I'm not afraid of you, Okeanos. I'm not disgusted. I want to know you. I want to love you, exactly as you are. My goddess sent you to me when I needed you most. Why would I turn you away now?"

:Because you don't need me any longer.: The bluntness of my response made me wince internally, but I couldn't help it. The touch of her small finger against me was making everything inside me writhe with interest. I could taste her skin, even through the smallest of my cups.

"But I do need you. I need every single one of my Blood. There are twenty or more eager Aima warriors standing outside my nest this very minute begging for an introduction, and that's after I already sent away the first dozen who were here earlier today. I don't want them. I don't need them."

:Why?: That single word vibrated and crashed inside my head.

"Because I have you. I want *you*. I *need* you. Exactly as you are."

SHARA

The giant sea monster of legend flinched away from me. Terrified that he might repulse me.

Me, his queen. Even after he'd saved me. Even after I'd freed him.

I wasn't angry or hurt—just sad. Sad that he'd never had anyone in his entire life who'd loved him exactly as he was. Who'd cared whether he lived or died. Who'd wanted him to be free, rather than trapped in a cramped cell at the bottom of a fucking koi pond.

I'd thought that getting into the water with him might help, but he'd retreated as far as he could, given his huge size and the comparably small pool.

I turned my hand palm up, stretching out my other fingers so I could touch more of the dangling tentacles. "Why are these smaller? They're almost like a beard."

:More dexterous. The better to catch any fleeing small prey or bits of shark or whale that might fall out of my beak.:

I didn't need to listen to his bond to know that he was trying to scare me off. He didn't *want* me to get closer to him. Only because it would hurt more when he lost me. When I sent him back to the cage.

I lifted my other hand toward his lower… jaw. Or chin area, though his head was definitely not humanoid. He wasn't slimy at all, despite the way his skin shone in the

water. He felt more like leather. Like Leviathan's hide—
without the scales. "You're basically a dragon of the ocean."

:I fucking beg your pardon,: Mehen roared in my head.
:What the everloving shit did I do to deserve such an insult?:

"Don't mind him." I laughed softly, letting the water carry
me closer to Okeanos. "He's still mad that Guillaume calls
him a lizard."

One of the thicker tentacles was drawn up tight to his
body, almost like a stepping stone out of the water. I braced
my foot on that ledge and stepped up closer to him.

Then I sat on that folded up tentacle like it was a root or
limb of my tree.

He made a gurgling sound that I was pretty sure was
choking, not laughing. Perhaps he was going into anaphy-
lactic shock.

Ignoring his reaction, I leaned back against his body,
exactly the same as I would have done with Rik or any of my
Blood. He wasn't exactly cuddly like Daire, but I'd leaned
against Leviathan before. He'd curled his scaly hide around
me, and I hadn't flipped out and lost my shit. But Okeanos
hadn't ever seen me like that with any of my Blood in their
monster forms. In fact... he might not even know much
about my other Blood, let alone *my* other forms.

"I've shifted into a cobra queen and a wyvern, but nothing
that could swim. How long do you think I could hold my
breath as an Aima queen?"

He opened his huge mouth enough to let me glimpse the
jagged rows of teeth inside. As if he truly thought he could
answer me with words. Then he must have caught himself,
clamping his mouth shut so as not to make me fear he was
going to toss me back into that maw and devour me in one
easy bite. *:I have no idea, my queen.:*

"Do you think I could swim along with you sometime? Or
would the water pressure kill me?"

:You wouldn't be able to reach the deep blue, unless you can transform into something like me.:

"Is the water really blue that deep?" I let wistfulness echo in my tone. "I bet it's beautiful."

:I don't exactly see colors.:

"Really? Then why do you call it the deep blue?"

He shrugged, a very human-like gesture that made several of the larger tentacles unfurl slightly as he relaxed. *:It feels blue.:*

"What do I feel like?"

He was silent a moment, but I was pleased to feel his body softening against my back. He wasn't trembling against the rocks any longer. *:Love. You feel like love and home.:*

I swallowed hard and rubbed the back of my head lightly against him. "Good. I am your home, Okeanos. I want you to be safe and happy with me."

:I know you couldn't love me like them, but...:

His words stumbled to a halt as I turned to look up into his eyes. "I love you now, Okeanos, and that love will only grow as we spend more time together."

His black eyes glistened like spilled ink. *:How could you love a monster like me?:*

I ran my hand over the muscled strength of the thick tentacle gripping the ledge behind my head. "All of my Blood are monsters. My father is the god of monsters. *I* am the biggest monster of all. Of course I love you."

Even... like this?

He didn't say the words, even in our bond, but I felt them thundering in his mind.

Very deliberately, I pressed my body against his, flattening my breasts against him. I deliberately shifted my weight so I started to slide off my tentacle seat.

And he caught me, a tentacle ever so gently winding around my waist to keep me from falling back into the water.

I didn't try to school my reactions. I allowed my eyes to flare with surprise at the sensation, squirming a little. "It tickles. It feels like mouths. Can you taste me?"

His coloring lightened, from midnight black and deep indigo to delicate lavender. *:They're not mouths, but yes, I do taste you. I taste you everywhere through my skin.:*

I laid my head against his body, listening for his heartbeat. I heard a deep, sonorous echo inside him, but it came from several directions.

:I have three hearts.:

No wonder the pounding seemed to fill his entire body. As I laid against him, relaxed and unafraid, he slowly began to touch me. Hesitantly at first, the slightest brush of one tip against my hair. A tickling dance across my back. When I didn't draw away or rebuke him, he very carefully wrapped his tentacles around me.

Hugging me to him.

Just holding me.

I lost track of time, relaxing in his embrace. We drifted, floating and gently rocking. I wasn't surprised to find that the grotto had disappeared, though I hadn't deliberately opened the sea portal. I hadn't felt us passing through and we certainly hadn't gone underwater. It was going to take some time and experimentation for me to figure out how to control the portal inside the grotto.

Rik's bond was a heavy presence in the back of my mind, intensely alert now that I was so far from him, but he understood my need to reassure my newest Blood. Okeanos needed some time alone with me. He needed to feel safe and comfortable with me, even if that meant floating on an ocean thousands of miles from my nest.

Flattening out his body, Okeanos rolled slightly so I was on top of him like a raft. I leaned up enough to look around. A beautiful island jutted up out of cerulean waters. Pure white sand glistened in the sunlight. A structure rose out of the middle of the island, but I didn't know what it was. Not a building—though it had regular and symmetric architecture. It looked like a natural part of the environment, almost like cliffs and mountains, but it was pink and orange in color.

:*Undina built her nest from living coral.*:

Oh shit. He'd brought me to his mother's nest—without telling her a queen was invading her territory? I started to jerk upright but then remembered I didn't have on any clothes. Maybe it'd be best if I stayed low.

:*She's coming.*:

Great. Just great. :*If I'd known we were going to see your mother, I'd at least put on a robe or something.*:

For the first time, my kraken laughed. His gills fluttered gently, and water spurted from his beak, or snout. Mouth. Whatever it was.

A woman's head popped up out of the water nearby, making me jump. She was close enough for me to feel her power sparking on my skin... but not close enough to risk getting entangled by Okeanos' tentacles if he decided he needed a snack.

Blue hair the same color as the water hung about her face and shoulders in heavy strands almost like dreadlocks, only they flowed and fluttered about her. Scales the same pretty color dotted her throat, but she had full breasts and two arms like a woman. Something dark flashed beneath the surface of the water, a hint of glittering silver reflecting the light. Her tail swept up, breaking the surface of the water like a graceful dolphin.

"Greetings, House Isador." Her words were drawn out, echoing as if she spoke underwater. "Welcome to House Ketea."

Okeanos made several soft whistles that I didn't understand, but Undina nodded and smiled at me.

"Thank you for doing what I could not."

Anger sparked inside me. I'd seen enough of his memories to know that he'd had a fucking miserable childhood. She'd never been much of a mother to him. So what if he was a kraken. She was a fucking mermaid creature, and I was pretty sure her teeth were razor sharp and jagged, though I'd only caught a glimpse as she spoke.

I sat up, crossing my legs and shaking my wet hair back off my shoulders. So what if I was naked and sitting on top of a kraken. "He's mine now, and he'll never be caged or imprisoned again."

"As I said, thank you. I couldn't control him, even as a boy. I couldn't spare him the burden of his heritage. I would have rather borne a queen like your mother, but it wasn't meant to be. House Ketea will sink beneath the waves when I pass."

Grudgingly, I nodded, but I couldn't find it in me to feel sorry for her. Not after what she'd done to her own son. "Triskeles lives again."

Her eyes narrowed and her lips curled, baring those brutal sword teeth. "Excellent. Your mother was right, then. I'll tell the other Skolos queens. May we count you as an ally against the Triune?"

"Not exactly."

Her tail slapped against the water, though her face didn't change.

"We need all nine seats filled and we have to work together. Our goddesses need us."

She glared at me a moment longer and then nodded just as grudgingly as I had. "You've felt the coming storm, then."

"Do you know what it is?"

Her teeth flashed and she surged up out of the water like a sleek fish dancing across the water. "The Screaming Madness."

She dived beneath the water and disappeared, presumably swimming back to her nest. Maybe I'd misunderstood her. Screaming Madness? I didn't even know what that was. "Do you know what she meant?"

:*No, my queen. I've never heard such a phrase.*:

I sighed and looked up at the sky. The sun was setting into the ocean, leaking deep orange, pink and gold into the water as if the sun was melting. It was mesmerizing, watching the sky darken...

To the exact shades of purple and lavender of my kraken's tentacles that were still looped around me. Holding me so carefully.

I quirked my lips, letting my eyes grow heavy and sultry. "How slowly can you shift back to your human form?"

His tentacles tightened slightly, holding me closer... as if he was afraid of losing me. :*I've never been able to control the shift, my queen.*:

"Until now." I read his confusion in our bond and felt the tension coiling through his massive body. He was afraid I intended to ask him to do something that was impossible. One final test... that he'd ultimately fail.

He still thought his time with me would be brief. Though he was absolutely willing to try and do anything I asked.

"I want you to start shifting back to your human form so I can fuck you again. But I don't mind your tentacles."

He jerked beneath me, his entire body shimmying in the water. He couldn't even form words or thoughts in our bond. He hesitated, frozen, afraid to do something wrong when he didn't understand exactly what I wanted.

I pressed a kiss between his dark eyes and threaded my fingers in the smaller tentacles. "Show me what you can do with these tentacles as we pass back through to the grotto."

OKEANOS

I t had to be a trap. A test that I couldn't pass. Her request didn't make sense otherwise.

For a moment, blinding rage swept through me. The same rage that had driven me to level as much of Undina's nest as possible. Only this time, if I lost my queen...

I'd level the entire world. I'd destroy every human city on every coast before I'd go peacefully back to the cage.

But then her lips touched me. Voluntarily. I felt the flick of her tongue. My skin immediately absorbed her saliva, stirring a formidable hunger in me. I wanted to taste her blood through my skin. Even better if I could also taste her desire. She was so close. Open, unguarded, and unafraid.

If it was a trap...

Then so be it. I had to know. I had to feel her. Know her. As only I could.

I loosened my fierce grip on her, letting my tentacles unwind over her limbs. Her back. She sighed softly and sank deeper against my body, lying completely relaxed on my belly. Even when I carefully slipped a tentacle around her neck. Not to threaten her in any way—but I needed to know how serious she was about letting me touch her. No queen in her right mind would allow a kraken to seize her throat. Powerful or not, an Aima queen still needed air, and it would be ridiculously easy for me to snap off her head.

Yet my queen lifted her chin and allowed me to roll her over on her back on top of me. Baring her vulnerable stomach and the sweet curves of her breasts to my touch. Even when I deliberately placed a suction cup on top of her nipple, she didn't jerk away. She didn't rebuke me.

Her nipple hardened at my caress. She moaned softly. She

didn't fight to get away. Even as I wound around her arms and legs, pinning her carefully against me.

Her breathing quickened, but not in fear. Her bond was wide open to me. Anticipation unfurled inside her. Interest, a bit of titillation, but not dread or anxiety. Even as I hesitantly slipped the tip of my tentacle up her inner thigh.

"Can you taste me?" She whispered, rubbing the back of her head against me. "Do you feel how much I want you? Pierce me so you can taste my blood as you wished. Let me bleed on you."

Goddess below, her words ignited the creature even more. Some of my suction cups also had tiny needles inside. I could inject a paralytic into my prey, keeping them alive while I slowly devoured them.

She absorbed that nugget from my thoughts and still didn't jerk away from me. "I too can inject poison. I once envenomed Rik as the cobra queen and actually killed him as I feasted on his poisoned blood. As I told you before, I'm the biggest monster of all, yet he still loves me."

:As I love you. As we all love you.:

I released dozens of tiny needles into her arms. She shivered and moaned again, arching her back in offering. I brushed those tiny needles over her breasts, and she sucked in a quick breath. Her nipples were rock hard, aching in our bond. Her desire burned like a beacon in the darkening night, as if the dissolved heat of the sun flowed up inside her. Heating her blood to a boil as drops spilled onto my sensitive skin.

Water spouted from my jets. A thick cloud of ink spilled into the water around us. The pungent scent of my glands thickened the air.

Ink. Blood. Mixing in the water. Combining on my skin. For a moment, I lost all control. In a blood frenzy, I rolled like a crocodile, thrashing the water with my ecstasy. I took her beneath the water, wrapping her tighter so I could feast on her blood directly from the salty water.

Then I tasted something even sweeter. More addictive. More powerful.

A nectar with enough power to rise Atlantis back up from its watery grave.

My queen's desire.

I flattened the tentacle over her flesh, drinking in every drop. She wiggled against me, fighting my fierce hold on her, and something died in me.

The last fragile bit of hope I carried.

The sun sank beneath the ocean and night fell. Stark and dark and empty.

I stilled my frenzied rolling, making sure her head was up out of the water. I started to uncoil from her. She lifted her hips, moving closer to my touch. Not away. Adjusting herself until...

She cried out softly. The most wondrous sound I had ever heard in my entire life, even raised among the sirens of the deep.

I pressed that suction cup down harder on her clit. I found her nipples again, working them gently, cradling her against me as the stars came out to illuminate her skin. She groaned again, her hips undulating against me.

:I want to be filled.:

Her bond clamored inside my head, the words bouncing around like frantic birds. She'd wanted me to shift, but I didn't feel the human form anywhere close. I'd never been able to control it.

:I need you, Okeanos. Please.:

My siren. My angel. My savior. My queen.

Ever so gingerly, I pressed a tip to her delicate opening. She rocked her hips up, pushing me deeper, inviting me inside. Tentacles and all. She rode me, pulling me under.

Taking even the mighty kraken toward to the bottom of the ocean. I couldn't have saved myself if I'd tried.

The deep blue beckoned. And I sank like a stone with her tangled against me.

SHARA

Riding the last wave of climax shuddering through me, I pulled us through the portal, this time more aware of what I was doing. For a moment, the pressure crushed my lungs, but the most gorgeous color I'd ever seen was worth that bit of agony. The deep blue, as he called it, the same color as my kraken's eyes.

My head broke the surface, and I sucked in a deep breath of air. My grotto surrounded us once more, the air thick and heavy with steam. My kraken still clutched me to him, his tentacles coiled around me, feasting on me.

I rocked my hips again, groaning at the fullness inside me. Unlike a man's dick, his tentacle could expand and fill every crevice, adjusting to my exact size.

And then more, evidently, because I felt him... flex inside me. Filling me even more.

I held him inside me as he started to shift. I couldn't see, since he was behind me, but through our bond, I felt the kraken folding up inside him. Compressing and coiling up smaller as the man emerged. His arms clutched tightly around me. His heart thudded heavily against my back.

His dick balls-deep inside me rather than the tentacle.

I sank my fangs into the meaty muscle of his biceps wrapped around my throat and he let out a roar of release.

He lost his footing and we both slipped beneath the surface of the water again.

Rik snagged him by the nape and hauled him up on the rocks to pant and gasp, while I crawled up between them. My alpha wrapped his body around me, automatically doing a quick wellness check. I wasn't offended, because I'd been far, far away from him. He never liked letting me out of his sight.

"Goddess below." Okeanos groaned, blinking up at me. "I never thought you'd be able to do that. I think you almost drowned the kraken."

My cheeks pinkened, making Rik laugh. "It's a good thing Daire isn't here to mouth off something inappropriate."

Leviathan dropped down beside us, his tail lashing back and forth with mock fury, even as he laid his scaly head on my thigh. *:Fuck that shit. I'll make all the inappropriate innuendos if you'll take me to the bottom of the ocean next.:*

I rubbed his forehead and leaned back against Rik. Okeanos took my hand in his and kissed my knuckles. For the first time, I didn't sense any fear in him. Any doubt. Any hesitation in touching me as he wished.

Filled with peace and love, I smiled up at the moon and knew in my heart that the Great One smiled back.

My kraken was finally home where he belonged.

The End

6

AUTHOR'S NOTE

I hope you enjoyed this time with Shara and her Blood. Be sure to pick up Queen Takes Darkness, which gives you some clues to what the "Screaming Madness" is. If you've been waiting for more Princess Takes Unicorns, rejoice! I plan to continue Xochitl's story in the Magic and Mayhem boxed set.

I am still letting Shara's future brew in the back of my mind, along with the other queens who need to come to the table. Sometimes it takes a while for things to solidify in my mind, but I know that Shara will be returning after I get a few pieces moved around on the board.

If you're looking for something to read in the meantime, I do have a couple of completed series to check out. If you loved Game of Thrones, try The Shanhasson trilogy starting with The Rose of Shanhasson. Looking for contemporary BDSM? Try The Connaghers or Billionaires In Bondage, starting with The Billionaire Submissive.

I have a few new things I'm hoping to throw into the mix too. More to come!

Thank you as always for your support.
Long live House Isador!